K c Rx

⊗ l

D1606457

Dark Horse
A Story of the Flying U

Dark Horse

A Story of the Flying U

B.M. BOWER

Sagebrush
Large Print Westerns

Library of Congress Cataloging-in-Publication Data

Bower, B.M., 1874-1940
   Dark horse / B.M. Bower.
     p.   cm.
   ISBN 1-57490-366-7 (lg. print : hardcover)
   1. Ranch life—Fiction. 2. Large type books. I. Title

PS3503.O8193 D37 2001
813'.52—dc21   2001032059

Cataloging in Publication Data is available from
the British Library and the National Library of Australia.

Sagebrush Large Print Westerns are published in the United
States and Canada by Thomas T. Beeler, Publisher, PO Box 659,
Hampton Falls, New Hampshire 03844-0659. ISBN 1-57490-366-7

Published in the United Kingdom, Eire, and the Republic of
South Africa by Isis Publishing Ltd, 7 Centremead, Osney
Mead, Oxford OX2 0ES England. ISBN 0-7531-6452-3

Published in Australia and New Zealand by Bolinda Publishing
Pty Ltd, 17 Mohr Street, Tullamarine, Victoria, Australia, 3043
ISBN 1-74030-309-1

Manufactured by Sheridan Books in Chelsea, Michigan

THE LIGHTNING STRIKES

LOPING ALONG THE TRAIL THAT SCALLOPED OVER foothill ridges between Meeker's ranch and the Flying U, Big Medicine sweated and cursed the month of April for arrogating to itself the sultry heat of July. The cigarette he had rolled and lighted before mounting for the homeward ride was smoked to its stub. It did not seem worth while to light another. What Big Medicine craved most was a quart bottle of cold beer. Failing that, his thoughts kept recurring to the trickle of cold spring water down his gullet. Following that thought his head swung involuntarily to the left, where a faint stock trail angled down a barren ridge into One Man Coulee. And without any command to do so, his sorrel horse, Cheater, turned in response to the glance and began picking his way through rock rubble on that trail. A trivial incident on an unimportant ride; yet such are the inscrutable ways of destiny that the turning aside to drink from a certain spring he knew was not the small matter it seemed to Big Medicine. He was not the man to shy from anything in the trail he chose to ride; one glimpse into the future, and even the blatant courage of Big Medicine must certainly have fled the thing before him.

That glimpse was not offered. So Big Medicine and his sorrel horse, Cheater, went down into One Man Coulee and drank with an audible gusto from the spring seeping out beneath a bulging, moss-covered ledge: Big Medicine lying flat on his belly, mouth and sunburned .nose submerged in the clear pool, Cheater, fetlock deep in the ooze, knees bent while he sucked the cold water

1

avidly through flaccid lips and big yellow teeth. Big Medicine lifted his face to the blasting sun, stared at the heat waves radiating from the rock walls near by, and drank again. Then he pulled off his big Stetson and soused his bullet head three times to his collar. He got up gasping and blowing luxuriously, dragged Cheater back out of the mud where yellow jackets were crawling, made himself a cigarette and heaved himself reluctantly to the saddle.

From the spring his best trail lay down the coulee, following the narrow, brushy water-course to the gravelly road that cut across the coulee's mouth on its way to certain remote ranches and that forbidding wilderness known as the Badlands. Refreshed, the sorrel loped steadily down the grassy trail, rutted here and there with the passing of infrequent wagon wheels—but he could not lope fast enough to escape the thing into which Big Medicine's thirst had betrayed him, for when Destiny chooses to make use of a man, his least act will lead to the task appointed.

As he topped the hill leading out of the coulee, Big Medicine's pale, round eyes sent a startled glance toward the west. In the little while he had been hidden within the high walls of One Man Coulee a storm had rolled up from the sky line over toward Lonesome Prairie. Already a greenish gloom lay upon the land to the westward, and the hot breeze had died into a sinister silence so great that the cheep of a bird in a bush sent Cheater shying skittishly out of the road.

When Big Medicine's hand dropped to his horse's neck the hair crackled as in winter. His own skin prickled. The air seemed soaked with electricity. He sent an uneasy look around him and his mouth pulled down at the corners. He did not like the sullen way the lightning was lifting and

2

parting the sluggish roll of clouds up there. Deep, that storm was; deep and ugly; full of water. Full of wind too, and thunder and lightning. A ripsnorter, like you'd have a right to expect in July or August.

Big Medicine stopped Cheater, got off and untied his yellow slicker from behind the saddle. Smelled fishy, in all this heat, but he flapped himself into it, buttoned it to his chin, and remounted, pulling the peaked slicker tail well down over the cantle of his saddle and tucking the edges neatly under his legs. Never saw a meaner storm, not even in the Pecos country where cyclones would come and tear the grass right up by the roots. He yanked his big hat down tighter over his pale eyebrows, tilted his spurs to graze Cheater's sweaty flanks and rode grimly forward. No shelter close enough to do any good; he'd have to ride and let 'er rip.

He was a little dubious about Dry Gulch, which lay just ahead. Might come a cloudburst before he got through, and the banks were too shaley and steep to climb. Big Medicine had been caught in a cloudburst once, and the experience had left him leery of low ground in a storm. He'd have to chance it, though; which he did at a swift gallop, watching the approach of the storm he was riding to meet. And for the first time he wished he had not ridden down into One Man Coulee to that spring. Only for that he'd have this stretch of trail safely behind him, with high level prairie to travel.

Into the smothered stillness of Dry Gulch there came the faint drumming of strange hoofbeats ahead of him on the trail. Coming his way, the fellow was. Between the muttering of thunder he could hear his steady approach, and in another minute a lathery black horse galloped into sight around a bend, his rider jouncing in the saddle, one hand gripping the horn.

3

Big Medicine snorted his disdain of all pilgrims when there came an ear-splitting crash and a blinding glare. The wide grin wiped itself off his mouth. The black horse fell as if a giant hand had slapped him down. One glimpse he had of the rider pitching headfirst into a clump of weeds, as Cheater squatted and whirled back up the gulch. With an iron hand he fought the sorrel's stark terror, spurring him back to the spot. The stench of brimstone was in his nostrils. Frozen mice were dancing under his hat. His knees buckled under him when he dismounted, but the stern stuff of the Good Samaritan was woven into the fiber of Big Medicine's soul and he went forward, dragging Cheater stiff-legged at the end of the bridle reins.

Shore was funny, the way lightning acted. That one bolt shooting straight down, and the rest playing crack-the-whip up in the clouds till you couldn't hear yourself think. The black horse lay flat and shapeless, every bone in his body crunched, by the look of him. The pilgrim wasn't dead, though. Black as a nigger, except for his light hair, but there were no marks on him so far as Big Medicine could see, when he bent over the clawing figure in the weeds.

Big Medicine spoke to him, but the man went limp and still, lying on his face. He yelled another question, then stooped and lifted the fellow in his arms and staggered over to where Cheater stood rolling his eyes until the white showed all around.

"Don't yuh wall yer eyes at me," Big Medicine bellowed peremptorily. "You gotta pack double, from here to the ranch. Make up yer mind to it right now, by cripes!"

He reached for the dragging reins, caught the inert figure firmly under the arms, and heaved him up to the

4

saddle. At that instant the lightning ripped a blinding rent in the gloom, there came on the heels of it another deafening report, and the big sorrel ducked and was gone, legging it for home with his head held sidewise, so that he would not trip on the reins. Clods of sandy soil hurtled backward from his pounding hoofs.

In the crackle and roar of the storm Big Medicine stood and damned the horse as long as he was in sight. Then, because the stranger was still breathing and no man with a heart would leave him there to die, Big Medicine heaved and grunted and swore until the flaccid body was balanced across his shoulders like a fresh-killed buck. A fool's job, most likely. The fellow would probably die on the road, but Big Medicine could not help that. Since it was his damnable luck to ride along there and see the lightning strike, he'd have to do what he could to save the man's life. So he hitched his burden to a more perfect balance and started for home, walking bow-legged under the load and searching his memory for new and more blasting epithets which he applied to Cheater.

A gust of wind stopped him in the trail until its first fury was spent. Blinding thrusts of swordlike lightning lifted the hair on his bullet head. Thunder crashed above him and rolled sullenly away to give place to the next ear-splitting explosion. Before he had gone ten rods the rain came in a sudden deluge: gray slanting curtains of water blown stiffly against him, blotting out the yellow banks on either side. He, who had so lately craved cold water, walked through rain so dense he felt like a diver ploughing along at the bottom of the sea.

HERO FOR A NIGHT

THINKING UNEASILY OF CLOUDBURSTS, BIG MEDICINE almost trotted the two-mile stretch to the hill that spelled safety. Up the soapy incline he toiled, slipping and sweating and swearing but somehow never falling or stopping until he reached the top. He wished he had thought to take off his spurs before he started—but hell, a feller can't think of everything at once. He wished he had worn his old boots; these new ones made of his heels a flaming agony. But there was a new schoolma'am boarding at Meeker's, and a feller hated to ride in run-over boots.

While he trudged those weary miles, he sent furtive glances this way and that beneath the streaming brim of his big hat. If there were only some cut-bank with an over-hang—if there was a tree or a clump of bushes, even, he would lay the fellow down under shelter and go on after a rig to haul him in to the ranch. But there was no cut-bank, no tree, no clump of bushes on that level prairie.

Anyway, the boys shore would have to hand it to him for nerve, packing a long-geared son-of-a-gun like this feller all the way in from Dry Gulch. He'd bet there wasn't another one in the bunch that would have sand enough to tackle it, even. A growing pride in his strength and big-heartedness steadied his feet as they squashed along the rutted trail.

After that it suddenly occurred to him that a rescue party would probably ride into sight over the next ridge. The minute Cheater showed up at the ranch with an empty saddle the boys would pile onto their cayuses and start right out. They'd think he was struck by lightning

6

or something. By cripes, they shore would bug their eyes out when they saw him walking in with a man on his back, unconcerned as if he was packing a stick of dry wood to the fire. It pleased him to picture the look on the faces of the Flying U boys when they came galloping out to find him. It pleased him to invent careless phrases, telling of his prodigious deed. "Oh, jest a feller struck by lightnin' over in Dry Gulch. Hawse broke back on me—had to hoof it home."

But as he plodded mile after mile and no bobbing horsemen showed on the blurred horizon, his pale, frog eyes hardened perceptibly. By cripes, them lazy hounds had time enough to meet him with an ox team. Time enough to push a wheelbarrow to Dry Gulch, by cripes! Damn a bunch of selfish boneheads that'd set in the bunk-house and let a feller lay out on the range and rot, for all they knew or cared! He'd show 'em up, by cripes! He wouldn't say a word; just the bare fact of what he was man enough to do would show 'em up for what they was. Yellow-livered skunks—there wouldn't be a damn' one that could look him in the eye. He'd ride 'em to a fare-you-well for this.

The thunder and lightning slowly drew off, muttering, to the high canyons of the Bear Paws. When he reached the brow of the hill that formed the north wall of Flying U Coulee, the storm had diminished to a steady drizzle, deepening the murky gloom of early evening. As he toiled up from the willow-fringed creek, the sight of Cheater standing tail to the storm beside the stable made him grind his teeth in wrath beyond even his extensive vocabulary. One sweeping glare showed him other horses sheltered in the dry strip on the corral side of the stable. Not a saddle missing under the shed; everybody inside, dry and warm— and be damned to them! The light in the bunk-house window, shining yellow through the rain-washed dusk, taunted him like a leering face, but he was too near the end of his strength to do more than grunt at this final insult. With a rocking, sidewise gait he staggered up the path to the cabin, his failing energy gathering itself for one savage kick upon the closed door.

"Hey! Cut that out!" yelled a voice he recognized as Cal Emmett's.

"Say, wipe the mud off your feet! We scrubbed the floor to-day," admonished another.

Big Medicine bellowed anathema as he let go the dangling ankle of his load and threw open the door. The Happy Family, humped around a poker game, looked up with casual glances that steadied to a surprised interest. Pink straddled backward over a bench and came forward, his eyes big with questions, though he said nothing.

"Who's that?" blurted Slim unguardedly.

"Somebody hurt?" Weary swept in his cards and rose, recklessly scattering the piled matches.

"Hully gee!" Cal Emmett exclaimed, kicking over a chair in his haste to come forward.

"Git outa my way!" panted Big Medicine, tottering toward his bunk in a far corner. "By cripes, I wouldn't ast none of yuh to go to no trouble—you kin go to hell instid!" He turned himself about, leaned awkwardly to one side and let his limp burden slide to the blankets. With a great sigh born of exhaustion, he stooped creakily and lifted the lax legs to the bed. While the Happy Family stood huddled and staring, he shucked himself out of his slicker and flopped upon the opposite bunk, where he lay on the flat of his back, glaring contemptuously up at them.

"Don't do nothin' to save that pore feller's life," he implored with heavy sarcasm. "Gwan back and set down on yer damn' haunches an' let 'im die!"

8

Pink and Weary were already at the bunk, feeling the inert figure. Pink straightened from his ineffectual pawing and stared down at Big Medicine.

"What's the matter with him, Bud? There ain't any blood nor any broken bones on 'im—what is this; a frame-up?"

"Here, take a look at him, Mig." Weary stepped aside to make room for the Native Son, who had a certain deftness in ministering to the injured. "Darned if I can see anything wrong with him. Might be pickled, from the looks—only he lacks the breath of a drunk man."

"His pulse is making good speed," Miguel announced. "I think he is having one fine *siesta,* no?"

"*Siesta* my foot!" Big Medicine heaved himself to an elbow. "Honest to grandma, the taxpayers uh this county had oughta build 'em an idiots' home. They's a bunch uh candidates on this ranch it's a sin to let run loose. Why don't yuh *do* something? That pore feller's been lightnin' struck, by cripes! Let 'im lay there and *die,* will yuh? Never lift a hand—"

"Lightning struck?" Weary looked blankly from one to another.

"There ain't been any lightning to amount to anything for a couple of hours," Cal Emmett pointed out. "Don't try any Andy Green stunt on us, Big Medicine."

"No, by golly," Slim cut in; "one liar's enough in this outfit."

Big Medicine let down his feet to the floor and sat glaring from one to another.

"Over in Dry Gulch you kin find his hawse," he snarled. "If you lazy hounds had of took the trouble to come and see what had went wrong, when Cheater came in without me, I wouldn't a had to pack that pore feller clear from Dry Gulch on m' damn' back. His hawse—"

9

"Pulled out and left him?" Weary prompted.

"Killed. Busted every bone in his body. You kin ride over there t'morra mornin' and take a look. There ain't a feller on the ranch that's man enough to do what I done, by cripes! Packed that pore pilgrim eight mile, by cripes—"

"How d'you know he's a pilgrim?" Pink demanded suspiciously. "He ain't dressed like a pilgrim."

"No, by cripes, but I seen how he set on a hawse 'fore that streak uh lightnin' come at 'em. All right," he snorted disgustedly, as he lay down again, "let 'im lay there an' die, then! I packed 'im in, by cripes; I ain't goin' to nurse 'im back to health!"

"Well," Weary yielded, "he sure don't look like a sick man to me, but we'll take your word for it, Big Medicine. Get his shoes off, boys we better strip off these wet clothes and roll him in a hot blanket. Happy, you go up and see if the Old Man's got any brandy—the Little Doctor mighta left some in her medicine chest— and don't sample it on the way back!"

"Yeah, yuh might give me a jolt of it too," said Big Medicine, sitting up again with an eager look. "Shore is a fur piece from here to Dry Gulch—walkin' on foot with a back load like that there."

"Darned right," Weary agreed sympathetically. "Ain't every man could do it. Stick your foot up here and let me pull off them wet boots."

"Be darn careful, then," sighed Big Medicine. "I got blisters the size uh saddle blankets on both heels, by cripes!"

"Hully gee!" breathed Cal, sucking air through his teeth when the blisters were displayed to a sympathetic group of bent faces. "Anybody but you'd 'a' laid on his back and stuck his feet in the air and howled like a

10

whipped pup. We never dreamed you'd get set afoot, Bud. Anybody in the darn outfit but *you*."

"The best a riders has accidents," Big Medicine stated loftily. "It was hard goin', all right—but it was his life er my feet, and any man that *is* a man woulda done the same, I reckon. I'd 'a' packed 'im twicet as fur if necessary."

"Yeah, that's *you*," Pink gave admiring testimony, eyeing the injured feet with something approaching awe. For a cowpuncher set afoot is the most pitiable sight on the range, and blistered heels are more dreaded than bullet wounds. "You oughta soak them heels in carbolic before you get lockjaw or something."

"Haw-haw-haw-w-w!" chortled Big Medicine, his spirits lifted amazingly by admiration and two fingers of excellent brandy. "I'm the toughest ole wolf that ever howled along the Pecos River, by cripes! And the biggest-hearted. I saved a feller's life and I'm proud of it. Give 'im a shot uh that there brandy, and then I'll have another little snort. By cripes, I earnt it!"

The Happy Family agreed with him. With fine loyalty they first inspected the brandy, just to make sure that it was fit for medicinal purposes, and administered it sparingly to Big Medicine and the stranger brought within their gate. They glowed with pride in Big Medicine's achievement, in the greatness of his heart and in his fortitude. They felt a warm benignity toward the pilgrim, lying there flushed and speechless—but unmistakably alive—in Big Medicine's bunk. Until long past midnight a light shone into the drizzle through the two square windows of the Flying U bunk-house. Snatches of song, laughter, the cheerful confusion of voices raised in facetious argument overrode the drumming of rain on the low roof.

11

In a word, the Happy Family were for the time being in complete accord with Big Medicine and his splendid role of Good Samaritan. When at last they laid themselves between their blankets, the brandy flask had been emptied to the last drained drop—for medicinal purposes only—and Big Medicine was still wearing the warped halo of a saint (if one might believe the Happy Family's sleep-drugged statements). The rescued stranger was a hero also. Though his lips had not once opened for speech and nothing was known of his identity, they were for the time being perfectly willing to accept Big Medicine's optimistic statements and let it go at that.

Warm-hearted heroes all, they slept in happy ignorance of what the morrow might hold for them. Which was just as well.

FAME IS FLEETING

FAME IS A FICKLE THING, AS HAS OFTEN BEEN STATED and as Big Medicine straightway discovered. He went to bed a hero. He rose a man who has boasted overmuch and who must be put in his place and kept there. To a man the Happy Family snubbed him for the thing he had done; or which he claimed to have done. With slightly bloodshot eyes, they watched him ostentatiously salve his blistered heels, sucking his breath in through his teeth in a childish play for sympathy. They refused to be impressed.

"You'd think, by thunder, a man would have sense enough to buy boots to fit," Cal Emmett observed tartly to no one in particular.

"I never seen a man always trying to show off his

12

little feet, by golly, that had a lick uh sense," Slim growled agreement.

"They always suffer for it when they have to walk half a mile or so," Pink yawned.

"Yeah, I betcha Big Medicine never packed that guy a mile," Happy Jack declared sourly. "I've saw grand-stand plays before."

"If he did, it was just a mile too far," drawled the Native Son. "Tell yuh right now, I'd feel a darn sight more like booting him away from the ranch than packing him in here. He don't look so good to me, *amigos*."

"Well, damn the hull of yuh fer a hard-hearted bunch of booze hounds!" snarled Big Medicine, screwing his face into agonized grimaces while he slid his feet into his oldest boots. "Lapped up a hull quart of brandy the Little Doctor was keepin' fer medical cases like me 'n' that pore feller I brung home on m' damn' back! Lapped it up like a bunch uh sheep herders, by cripes! You wait—"

"You wasn't bashful about swillin' it down, yourself," Cal snorted. "We had to take a nip or two so we could stomach your darned bragging."

"Braggin'! Me? Well, by cripes!" Big Medicine sat on the edge of his bunk and goggled amazedly around at the disgruntled group. "Me brag! Packed 'im a mile, hunh? I dare the bunch of yuh to ride over to Dry Gulch and see where I packed 'im from, and then say ag'in that I packed 'im a mile, mebby."

"Don't worry—that's right where we're heading for, soon as we eat," drawled Weary. "If you packed that man on your back clear from Dry Gulch, my hat is off to you. You can brag about it for the rest of your life, for all me."

So a truce was tacitly declared for the time being.

"By golly, looks like he done it, all right," Slim admitted reluctantly an hour later, pointing a gloved finger toward drying footprints in the trail.

"Shore, I done it." Big Medicine, riding his chastened sorrel at the head of the little cavalcade, twisted in the saddle to glare back at the group. "It don't take my tracks in the mud to show I done it, either. My word for it had oughta be sufficient, by cripes!" He lifted an arm and gestured accusingly toward the faraway broken line of low ridges that marked Dry Gulch. "Six mile acrost this bench and two mile down the gulch, and I hoofed it every step uh the way with that pore feller on m' back. And you darned chumps settin' there in the bunk-house lettin' me do it!"

"Yeah, we heard that before," Pink reminded him.

"Hunh?"

"It was mentioned, *amigo*, seventeen times last night, and four times since we left the corral," the Native Son reminded him gently.

"Well, it's the truth, by cripes," Big Medicine bellowed over his shoulder. "When a man's hawse shows up with a empty saddle, it's time somebuddy rode out to see what took place. I coulda laid out here and *died*, by cripes!" His pale stare went from face to face. "That gits me."

"Aw, gwan!" snorted Happy Jack. "There wouldn't nothin' git you. I betcha a double-bitted axe wouldn't only show a few nicks if a feller tried to brain yuh with it. I betcha sparks'd fly off your head like hackin' at a rock. You wouldn't lay out an' die nowhere!"

"Wonder who that fellow is," Weary tactfully observed. "Not a thing in his pockets to show where he come from or where he was headed for. Cadwalloper and I went through his clothes and we didn't find the scratch of a pen."

"I betcha he's on the dodge," Happy Jack hazarded, with his usual pessimism. "He's got a mean look, to me."

"So'd you have a mean look, if you was struck by lightning," Big Medicine defended loudly. "The pore feller ain't goin' to be pesticated about no pedigree. He's all right—barrin' he don't know how to set a hawse. Pullin' leather with all two hands, and his hawse only in a high lope—but hell, that ain't no crime." He sent another sweeping stare over his shoulder. "I've saw as pore ridin' more'n once, right in Flying U Coulee."

"Who, for instance?" Cal Emmett demanded quickly.

Big Medicine hedged. "Well, I ain't namin' no names but I could shore spit in the feller's eye right now that I seen chokin' his saddle horn one mornin'—"

They disputed that assertion with bitter argument, while over their heads gray curlews sailed with slim legs dangling, curved rapier beaks thrust out as they called "Cor-reck? Cor-reck?" in aimless inquiry. On storm-draggled bushes, meadowlarks teetered and sang sweet snatches of rippling melody, endlessly repeated as if they had forgotten the rest of the song. These things, while seemingly unregarded, nevertheless soothed their mood appreciably.

"Oh, I forgot to say the Meekers aim to drive over t'day if the weather's good," Big Medicine announced suddenly, forgetting his grievance as they rode into Dry Gulch. "The new schoolma'am never has saw any real bronk ridin', so when Joe made a remark about ridin' over to watch me gentle that gray outlaw, schoolma'am spoke up an' said she wanted to come. So they kinda framed up a Sunday picnic over t' our place."

15

"Hully gee, I guess lightnin' musta struck you instead of that pilgrim," Cal Emmett grinned. "Why didn't yuh say they was comin'? I'd 'a' rode over to Bert Rogers' place—"

"Time enough yet, if you hurry," Weary pointed out. "Happy, you might drift on over to Adamses and get Len, if she's home. And you might swing around by Pilgreen's—"

"Aw the Pilgreens' is comin' anyway, if the old lady gits over her toothache," Happy Jack cut in unwarily.

"Oh. So *that's* where you was all yesterday forenoon! Lucky for you, ole timer, that Chip ain't back yet."

"Chip better git a wiggle on, by golly!" Slim cast an appraising glance out over the rolling hills, now brightly tinted with the green of new grass. "That there hot spell's shore puttin' grass on them hills."

"Andy oughta be rollin' in to-day or tomorrow," Pink observed rather wishfully. "There's a few snuffy ones in that last bunch we gathered that I'd sure like to see Andy go up against."

"Why? Want all them nice new fillings jarred loose outa his teeth?"

"By golly, the way he talked 'fore he left, Andy'll come home packin' enough gold in his mouth to start a bank!" Slim chortled. "Swaller all that and we'd have to beef 'im to git it back."

"By the looks of that last bunch, Andy's gold fillings ain't the only things liable to get jarred loose," Weary predicted, with a laugh. "Come on, boys—let's get this inquest over and done with. How much farther is it, Big Medicine?"

"Right around that next turn." Big Medicine reined importantly in the lead and went galloping down the gulch to where the dead horse lay. The Happy Family,

16

dismounting at the spot, gathered in a silent, staring group.

"What I can't *sabe* is how that guy at the ranch escaped with a whole bone in his body," Weary observed soberly at last.

"Well, he wasn't touchin' nothin' but the horn and stirrups when she struck," Big Medicine explained. "Prob'ly the lightnin' slid in under 'im. Yuh might say that's oncet a feller's life was saved by his pore ridin'. If he'd been settin' in the saddle like a human, he'd be playin' a harp right now, chances is, and wonderin' how he got there."

"Moral, ride high and loose in a thunderstorm," Pink declared in his clear treble.

"Say, I know that horse," Cal suddenly exclaimed. "I sure remember that bob-wire scar on the shoulder. That horse come from the livery stable in Dry Lake. Grab a leg, boys, and turn him over. We oughta pull the saddle, anyway."

They heaved the carcass to the other side, bringing the branded hip uppermost.

"Yeah, I could swore that was the horse," Cal confirmed his first statement. "That's the cayuse I rode to Box Elder after that locoed roan son-of-a-gun last spring, the time he busted his bridle and got away. Hard-gaited as the devil. I ain't surprised that pilgrim was anchored to the saddle horn. I know my back bone like to punched a hole in my hat before I'd rode this old pelter a mile."

"Well, the pilgrim's got no kick coming, at that. He's alive and the horse ain't. Better take his outfit back to the ranch, hadn't we?" Pink stopped and untied the small, leather bag that had evidently seen more hard usage than the storm would account for. The Happy Family gravely inspected it, discovered that it was

17

locked and handed it over to Big Medicine as the natural guardian of the fellow's belongings.

They removed the saddle and bridle from the dead horse, discussed the advisability of dragging the repulsive carcass off somewhere out of sight and smell of the road, and decided against doing it. For one thing, it would take a little time and they were in a hurry. For another, Weary raised the point of legal requirements. It might be wise, he thought, to leave the animal where it fell, so that the owner would have evidence of the manner of its death. Only lightning could work such havoc on bones without a surface mark. It might be important. Anyway, there was room to drive around the carcass, and they could come back later and drag it off.

All of which had a certain bearing on later developments, as they were soon to discover.

THE UNWELCOME GUEST

THESE SEEMINGLY SMALL MATTERS DISPOSED OF TO their satisfaction, the Happy Family rode cheerfully homeward; all, that is, save Happy Jack, who galloped away on a narrow stock trail which led by a short cut to the Adams ranch and on up to Jackson's; and Cal Emmett, who turned off at the upper gate on his way to bring Bert Rogers.

With a hundred and more horses fresh from the range and needing to know that man is master, no preparation for a bronk-riding contest was necessary. Give them an appreciative audience roosting on the top rails of the corral, and Monday's hard work would become Sunday afternoon's sport. They'd coax old Patsy to cook up a flock of blueberry pies and make plenty of coffee, and it would be a real picnic. Maybe some of the women would object to dancing that evening, on account of its being Sunday, but even old lady Jackson, who was said to be a member of the Baptist Church back East somewhere, allowed Rena to play games on Sunday. The Happy Family decided that there would be plenty doing, and if it didn't rain again, there would be a full moon for good measure.

"If Bert'll ride that Flopper horse of his over, I might give him a race with Glory. Any money in this crowd?" planned Weary.

Whereupon Slim had a sudden thought that brought a queer look into his eyes.

"Say, Weary, mebby I oughta told yuh b'fore—but that red-headed cousin of Bert's is out here ag'in. Bert told me in town. You want to keep yer eye peeled."

Certain men in the group had never heard of Bert Rogers' cousin, who had caused Weary more trouble than one woman has any right to cause. Those who did not know the story asked questions which Slim, rolling uneasy eyes toward Weary, blunderingly tried to parry. Then suddenly Weary laughed and turned to face them.

"Ancient history, boys. Myrt Forsyth and I went to school together back in Chadville, Iowa, and I got a bad case of calf love over her. Then I got the notion she was double-crossing me, so I pulled out and came west. I never knew she was Bert's cousin till she showed up out here at a dance in Dry Lake. I was all cured long ago, but mamma! It's women that taught cats how to deal a mouse misery. Myrt—" For once Weary hesitated, groping for words.

"Shore, we know the rest." Big Medicine laughed. "You went and had a relapse."

Weary flashed a glance at him.

19

"That's just the trouble; I didn't. No woman—some women—never can seem to realize a man can fall out of love as easy as he falls in. Myrt wasn't to blame, I guess, for trying a little spite work when she found out I wasn't packing any busted heart on her account. She's all right—"

"Aw, why don't you tell the truth about 'er?" Slim growled. "How she went an' lied about yuh, and tried to bust up you 'n' Miss Satterly—an' did, by golly! I always thought that was at the bottom of her pullin' out fer home—"

"I don't know as that's important right now," Weary rebuffed him. "The point is, Myrt Forsyth's here, and it's likely she's forgotten the whole thing. I know I have, just about."

Whereupon Slim twisted his bulky torso in the saddle and lowered a fat eyelid at the others.

"Fergive and fergit is what the Good Book says," he stated sententiously. "I don't guess it'll spoil your riding any to have Myrt Forsyth hangin' over the top rail watchin' yuh."

"Not what you could notice," Weary grinned. "I'm going to try that glass-eye sorrel a whirl; the one that come up in that bunch from Wyoming."

"Did you notice the spur marks on him?" the Native Son inquired. "But no mark of the saddle. A bad sign, *amigo*."

"All signs are bad when you ease your saddle up on a bronk's middle," Weary retorted. "Yes, he looks about as snaky as anything in the bunch. If I don't gentle him down, some of you boys are liable to get hurt; and it's too close to round-up to let you take a chance."

As Weary intended, the talk ranged far from girls and broken romances after that. Even the pilgrim was forgotten until they dismounted at the stable and hung the town saddle by one stirrup on a spare peg in the

20

shed. The Native Son untied the small black satchel from behind his cantle and held it up with a peculiar light in his eyes.

"Has it struck you fellows as being just a little peculiar, our unexpected guest heading into the Badlands in such a hurry with only this little bag?" he asked. "A locked bag." He looked at Big Medicine. "Before we go up to the bunk-house again, I think you ought to know that I caught him watching us on the sly and taking in every word we said about him."

"Say, when was that?" Big Medicine demanded with some resentment in his voice. "If yuh're tryin' to make out he was playin' me fer a sucker—"

"I didn't say that. It was when you kicked my boots back under the bunk, Pink, and I was down on the floor fishing them out. That *hombre* was watching you fellows like a trapped coyote. I saw his eyes turning from one to another through the slit of his eyelids. He was supposed to be unconscious, you remember. It was when Big Medicine was trying to convince us we ought to haul him to a doctor."

"That was before breakfast," said Pink, grinning a little.

"He got better, right away," Miguel added drily. "Asked for some coffee, you remember, and said he didn't feel so bad, only he had a head on him like the morning after, and he guessed he'd stay in bed to-day. Remember?"

"That's right."

"Say!" bawled Big Medicine angrily. "What yuh tryin' to make out? That pore feller never knowed what hit 'im, by cripes! When he woke up and found himself in a strange place this mornin', he just nacherly wanted to size up the layout 'fore he let on he was awake. I'd do the same thing m'self."

"They's something to that, all right," Slim agreed, looking from one to the other, wondering which side to take. "By golly, it was a tough-sounding bunch this mornin'."

"Yes, but there's something off-color in the whole thing," Miguel persisted, forgetting his little Spanish mannerisms, as he did when he was very much in earnest. "Why would a tenderfoot hire a livery horse and go pelting into the Badlands? That horse was a lather of sweat when he was struck dead. Didn't you boys notice it when we turned him over? Where the rain didn't wash off the dried sweat, it showed plain as day. And in a twenty-mile ride a man doesn't get saddle-galled like that *hombre* was— unless he's been hitting a fast pace."

"By golly, that's right," Slim admitted. "I never seen a man's legs skun any worse."

"Well, what's the answer, Mig?" Weary looked up from rolling a cigarette.

"*Quien Sabe?*" The Native Son shrugged as he reached for the tobacco sack dangling by its string from Weary's teeth.

"I s'pose yuh want 'im kicked off'n the ranch jest because he ain't got any sense about ridin' a hawse!" Big Medicine flung at him disgustedly. "Honest to grandma, I never seen such a suspicious feller as you are, Mig."

"All right, have it your way. Just the same, if you didn't pack a load of trouble into this coulee last night, I'll be surprised."

"Well, he can't steal any of *my* money," Pink observed philosophically. "I lost m' last two-bit piece on that full house of Slims, just before our brave hero came staggering into our midst with the dying man on his shoulders. I'm safely broke, thank God."

"The dying man could have walked in if he'd wanted to," the Native Son tersely declared. "I kinda thought last night he was playing possum to a certain extent. This morning—"

"This mornin' you're goin' to get the livin' tar knocked outa yuh!" bawled Big Medicine, who was nothing if not loyal to what he considered his responsibility. "That feller ain't able to knock them words down yore throat, but I am, by cripes!" While he talked, he began peeling off his coat.

"All right, if that's the way you feel about it. I tell you now, and time will prove it—that *hombre* is a crook. He'll deal you dirt, you mark my words. He's got about as much gratitude as a rattlesnake. Now, come on and fight!" The Native Son yanked off his new gray sombrero with its fancy silver-inlaid band and horsehair tassels, stepped into a clear space and put his hands in the significant posture of a trained boxer. Big Medicine rushed at him, grinding his teeth, but like a cat Pink leaped and landed on his back, wrapping arms and legs around him and clinging there like a leech. Weary stepped in close to the Native Son.

"Cut it out, Mig. You fellows'll need your energy for those bronks you're due to tackle before long. To-morrow morning, if you still want to tear each other apart, we'll all get up early and let you go to it. But folks are coming here to-day for a good time. If this is your idea—"

"Oh, forget it!" snapped the Native Son, reaching for his hat. "I admit this is a poor time to call the turn. But tomorrow morning I'll sure as hell show this frog-face Samaritan where he heads in."

Big Medicine halted in the act of pulling on his coat.

"And I'll learn a greaser to keep his mouth shut!" He started forward belligerently.

The insult turned Miguel's face livid with anger. He whirled to do battle, met Weary's steadying gaze and shrugged. Some one was driving briskly up the creek road, the rattle of the wagon sounding loud on the rocks as the horses splashed through the shallow ford. Miguel sent one hostile glance toward Big Medicine and picked up his rope, turning toward the corral. Even so, Weary did not appear satisfied. He followed Miguel through the gate, talking earnestly in an undertone, his hand on Miguel's shoulder.

"*Now* what they framin'?" Big Medicine twitched his coat into place and started for the two. "I'll beat the liver outa both of 'em in a holy minute, if they start framin' on *me!*"

"Aw, come back here!" Pink clutched his arm. "Weary's just calming Mig down. What you go and call him a greaser for? Don't you know he won't stand for that kinda talk? He's liable to knife yuh for it."

"Well, damn'im, he called me a Samaritan! There's some things I don't stand from no man!" Big Medicine lunged toward the gate.

"Aw, that's a compliment, you bonehead!" Pink tightened his grip.

"Like hell!" snorted Big Medicine, forging to the gate and dragging Pink with him.

"Sure, it is. Samaritan means helpful cuss same as the word pinto means a spotted horse. You ask Weary."

Big Medicine slowed, staring doubtfully after the Native Son.

"Well, I wish, by cripes, Mig would stick to plain United States," he grumbled. "That's no way to carry on an argument—draggin' in Mex words a feller never heard before." He grinned suddenly at Pink. "Little One, you saved Mig's life, by cripes!"

"All right, that makes me a Samaritan too," dimpled Pink. "Hey, Weary! Here's the Pilgreens!"

A lumber wagon came rattling into the yard and stopped a dozen feet from the shed, and with the clannishness for which the Happy Family was noted, the boys came grinning to welcome these neighbors whom no one save Happy Jack particularly liked. Mr. and Mrs. Pilgreen, with their listless daughter, Annie, occupied the lopsided front seat. Behind them on two quilt-cushioned boards laid across the wagon box rode five juvenile Pilgreens of assorted sizes. All were grinning bashfully, save the old lady herself, whose beady eyes were roving here and there, seeking food for criticism.

"Well, now, how are yuh?" Big Medicine greeted them in his bellowing voice. "Storm any, down your way?"

"Some. Wasn't you boys gittin' ready to fight, a minute ago?" Mrs. Pilgreen looked hard at Big Medicine.

"Hunh? Fight? Not on your life!"

"I could hear you swearin' something awful, comin' up from the crick, and I saw you peelin' off your coat and shakin' your fist at somebuddy. I d' know what you'd call it but a fight." Mrs. Pilgreen eyed him coldly. "I don't approve of swearin', especially on Sunday. Or fightin', either."

"No, mom, you're dead right. We wasn't, though. We was jest joshin' an' actin' the fool. Can I help you down?"

"I clumb in without help and I can climb out the same way," the lady retorted, peering over the edge like a hen turkey inspecting a roost. "You help the young'ns."

But Weary, Miguel and Pink were already performing that service. Big Medicine assisted the lank and lifeless Annie to the ground, wondering what Happy Jack could see in her to like. For thanks, she smiled and swallowed

25

and looked at her feet, standing limply waiting for her waspish mother to make her clawing, backward descent over the wheel.

"Louise Bixby to home?" Mrs. Pilgreen flipped her calico skirt into place and glared at Big Medicine.

"Countess? Shore! Go right on up to the house. She come to git the house cleaned 'fore Chip and the Mrs. git home. She'll be tickled to see you folks."

"An' that's a lie, if I ever told one in m' life," he muttered later to Weary, watching the visitors go straggling through the big gate. "Guess I'll go take a look at the pilgrim. Come on, Mig. I git mad sometimes, but I'm reasonable, by cripes. I want you should see fer yourself the pore feller ain't runnin' no whizzer. I'm willin' you should prove yore case ag'in 'im. And if that ain't fair enough, what is?"

"That's fine with me, *amigo*." The Native Son swung into step with him and they went off together. Weary and Pink, watching them go, glanced at each other and grinned.

RED LOCO

ANDY GREEN, HAVING ARRIVED IN DRY LAKE ON THE noon train the day before, "caught a ride" within an hour to the Rogers ranch. From there to the Flying U transportation would be simple; a borrowed saddle horse could be returned at his convenience—or, the next day being Sunday, Bert would probably ride over with him and bring the horse back. And when Cal Emmett rode into the yard on Sunday morning with his invitation for Bert, Andy greeted him like a brother. Lady Luck, in Andy Green's opinion, might nearly always be depended upon to play him for a favorite.

26

"Yuh know, Cal, my brain has been turning somersaults trying to scheme some way to get a lovely bunch of red *loco* over to the ranch to-day," he confided. With one arm thrown affectionately over the neck of Cal's horse and with his hat pushed back from his forehead, Andy looked innocent and earnest as a schoolboy.

"Red *loco?*"

"Yeah. Bert's cousin's here on a visit from the East. You haven't seen her yet. Prettiest red hair you ever saw in your life. Complexion like rose leaves floatin' in sweet cream. Eyes—"

"Hull-ee gee!" Cal's eyes rounded into the baby stare his fellows knew of old. "You wanta drift clean over the ridge, old-timer. If yuh mean Myrt Forsyth, I know that bunch of poison weed to a fare-ye-well."

"That's her name. But man, oh, man! She sure ain't poison to me!" Andy looked as if he meant it. "Now I'll get to ride with her to the ranch. She can watch me tame a bronk. With them blue eyes of hers looking down from the top rail—man, I can gentle chain lightning till you can roll it up like barb wire!"

"*Loco* is right," observed Cal sententiously. "You've got it in your system and there's only one cure 't I know of." He grinned, and added in response to Andy's questioning look, "Go on till you get your belly full. If it don't kill yuh, you're cured."

"That's the kinda medicine I'm crying for," Andy declared boldly. "But what's eatin' on you, Cal? She says she was out here, awhile back. Did you fall for that little gal yourself and get turned down?"

"Never you mind what I done. Get a move on. The boys was hopin' you'd show up to-day—they've got a horse or two picked out for you to ride. Nice easy ones. You better git over there before they frame something on yuh." Cal turned away then to shake hands with a fragile-looking young woman with shining red hair waving distractingly around her Dresden china brow, and long, heavy-lidded blue eyes whose briefest glance was calculated to raise a man's pulse at least ten beats a minute.

"*Cal!*" she breathed, laying her free hand over his. "*You*, of all people!"

"Same to you, Myrt," Cal smiled down at her. "I sure never expected to see you this morning."

Andy Green watched the two with narrowed eyes. That hand clasp was too significant, their fingers loosened too reluctantly to please him. It seemed to hint vaguely at past tenderness which might flare up again with the slightest encouragement. Andy did not like it. No one at the Flying U had ever mentioned Bert Rogers' cousin. Knowing the Happy Family, it certainly was queer that none of the boys had ever joshed Cal about her. They did whenever he looked at a girl—why not Myrtle Forsyth?

The mystery nagged at Andy. The ride to Flying U Coulee was not what he had hoped for. Cal and Myrtle kept harking back to her first visit in a way that made him an outsider. After a wonderful evening with her, sitting in the bay window of the Rogers house watching the storm, with Myrtle squealing and clutching his arm whenever there came a flash of lightning, it did not look right to him that she should be all eyes for Cal this morning.

Though it might not be polite to "horn in" on their conversation, Andy owned a little streak of stubbornness. He would not let them pair off by themselves as he suspected they would do at the first chance, but rode right with them and broke in with questions about the boys and the ranch and all that had

28

happened since he had left ten days before. Not that he was so darned anxious to know; he'd get the news soon enough from the boys. But when Cal was answering his questions, he couldn't talk to Myrtle and gaze into those blue eyes of hers.

The trick served its purpose for the time being, and they heard all about Big Medicine's adventure. But that only gave Andy a new grievance. Myrt Forsyth sure wasted a lot of sympathy on the stranger; more than he had coming to him. All right to be sorry—but she needn't have called him "that poor, poor boy" so often. The one cheerful note was that Cal was getting sore about it too.

For this reason Andy Green was not in his normal sunny humor when he left the two at the corral where the Happy Family were fore-gathered and rode on up to the White House with a letter for the Countess which was marked *Important, Rush!* in the Little Doctor's well-known handwriting.

"Keep away from that horse's heels," he paused to admonish a small Pilgreen child, who ran down the steps as he was about to enter the kitchen. "He'll lam your head off!"

"I wanta ride! Can I have a ride?" Two other young Pilgreens were converging upon the horse.

"No, you can't. Keep away, now. He'll take an ear off you in a minute." Scowling, Andy waited until they had withdrawn a little, then walked inside. The Countess rose from looking into her oven, gave him a harassed frown and beckoned him into her immaculate pantry.

"What under the shinin' sun am I goin' to do with them kids?" she demanded accusingly. "They've been here an hour, and I'd ruther have the locusts of Egypt devourin' the land."

"I dunno. What did Moses do with the locusts?" Andy looked up from searching for the Little Doctor's letter among a conglomeration of papers such as men carry for no reason whatever in their inside coat pockets.

"I'm a Christian woman, but if I don't feed them kids poison fly paper before the day's over—"

"Think it would work?" Andy grinned and returned to his search. In his present mood he could sympathize with the Countess as never before.

"Something's got to. You're so good at thinkin' up tricks, I should think you could do something. That old woman'll drive me to murder, if the kids don't." She listened through the closed door, heard the crash of falling tinware in the kitchen and gave Andy one desperate look as she rushed out. Having found the letter he was seeking, Andy helped himself to a doughnut from a two-gallon stone jar and went out, taking large bites.

"Gimme a doughnut. I wanta doughnut! Maw, can't I have a doughnut?"

Andy ate fast, moving forward in the midst of beseeching young Pilgreens. As the last crisp morsel disappeared down his throat, he reached the Countess. Through the open doorway Mrs. Pilgreen could be seen in the living room, solemnly rocking, with her hands folded in unaccustomed idleness across her starched white apron. Andy gave her one swift, appraising look. An overworked ranch woman on a Sunday visit is pretty hard to dislodge, as he had long ago learned from observation, but there was something in her personality that grated on his nerves. He turned to the Countess and said, in a voice pitched to carry above the clamor of young voices "Here's a letter from Mrs. Chip.

30

Somebody ought to telegraph Chip not to bring her and the kid home yet. With smallpox on the ranch—"

In the living room Mrs. Pilgreen had stopped rocking. The Countess gasped, caught Andy's look and nodded.

"I don't know what under the shinin' sun we're goin' to do," she complained fretfully. "D' you s'pose that pore feller they brought in last night—"

"It's a wonder he ever got this far. They're all stirred up over it in town. Worst case—"

There was a swish of starched calico, and Mrs. Pilgreen stood glaring in the doorway. Behind her stood Annie, her listless blue eyes wider than Andy had ever seen them.

"Louise Bixby, d' you mean to tell me there's smallpox on this ranch and we was let to come here without a word bein' said?" The old lady's eyes glittered as they darted quick glances from one to the other.

"You come of your own accord," snapped the Countess. "I'm sure I never asked you."

"You'd let us expose these innocent children without a word of warnin'. Annie, you get them kids' bunnits on 'em, quick. Alviry, you run tight as you can and tell your paw we're goin' home this minute."

More was said, to which Andy Green listened with a lifting of his spirits. Through the window he watched the departure. More than ever Mrs. Pilgreen resembled a hen turkey anxiously hustling her brood in out of the wet. The Countess, waiting until they were well through the big gate, turned then upon Andy Green.

"The Bible says a tongue without a bridle on is worse than a runaway horse, and I guess it's so," she snorted. "Why under the shinin' sun couldn't you think up something besides that? Lyin' outa whole cloth—she'll

31

backbite this bunch for the rest of the summer. I should think you'd be afraid the wrath of the Lord'd fall upon yuh for talkin' that way." But the twinkle in her near-sighted blue eyes softened the rebuke.

"Oh, I don't know." Andy pushed back his hat and ran his fingers absently through his hair where it was inclined to curl at the temples. "I did hear something about smallpox in town. Jimmy Myers at the store was talkin' about it while he was loading the groceries for Rogers. They've got a case, or think they have. Jimmy was kiddin' old Rogers about layin' in a supply because he'd be scared to show up in town again for a month. I didn't get the straight of it—Jimmy's an awful liar. But I wasn't lyin' outa whole cloth, Countess. And anyway, it worked."

"It's workin' like a jug of yeast," the Countess complained, glancing uneasily down the path. " 'Tain't much to start with, but if it's left long enough, it'll be all over the suller. Let Sary Pilgreen tell that yarn a few times and she'll have us all dead and buried and the coroner settin' on us. Seems to me you coulda thought up something that wouldn't spread so easy. I d'know but what, if I slapped one of them kids, it woulda had the same identical effect of startin' 'em fer home and she wouldn't find so much to talk about!"

"Well, by gracious!" Andy exclaimed, in a hurt tone. "If there's no gratitude around this ranch, how about another doughnut? They certainly are fine; about as good as I ever laid a lip across."

The Countess succumbed to the flattery and gave him three, which Andy strung neatly on the butt end of his quirt, the Countess scolding him continuously. She told him to get along out of the kitchen or she wouldn't have a crumb of anything left, and she pinched her lips tightly together to keep from smiling at him. So Andy

32

mounted and rode down to the bunk house—a distance of about fifty yards—carrying the quirt like a spear. He dismounted there and went in after his chaps, spurs and a new silk neckerchief. As he stood before the uneven square of broken bar mirror, adjusting the shining folds of blue silk around his throat, he suddenly decided that he needed a shave. Anyway, the Pilgreens might not have left yet, and it would do no harm to wait awhile before he showed up at the stable. And this thought reminded him to take a look at the lightning-struck jasper Big Medicine had carried all the way from Dry Gulch.

Andy pivoted slowly, scanning each bed as he turned. He had the bunk-house to himself. The fellow couldn't be much hurt, after all. With a sudden chill running down his spine, Andy stepped back to where he could crane through a window and see the trail where it left the stable yard. If old lady Pilgreen saw that fellow walking around—but no, there they went, driving off in their lumber wagon, the Happy Family with Myrtle Forsyth watching them go. Andy's eyesight was keen, but to satisfy himself, he made a deliberate count of the figures down there. No sign of the pilgrim anywhere. Then, just as he was turning away puzzled, he saw the fellow emerge from the mess house a few rods away and go down the path, walking wide, as a man will do who has saddle sores to think about.

Andy grinned in complete understanding. He knew that gait and all that it implied. He watched until the group at the stable turned to receive the stranger and moved on toward the corral out of sight, then got his white enamel shaving cup and ducked across to the mess house to beg hot water from old Patsy. Though he would not admit to himself that he felt any uneasiness

33

whatever over the competition foreshadowed down there, he wasted no seconds after that.

Smooth and bearing a faint odor of bay rum, Andy pinched his gray hat crown into the creases he favored most, set it upon his fresh-combed brown hair at a jaunty angle which he also especially favored, pulled his chap belt into position, stepped into the saddle and rode leisurely down the slope, munching the third doughnut as he went along and looking very well satisfied with life.

His reception was all that he hoped it would be. Myrtle Forsyth, standing on the rear end of a hayrack backed against the corral, was clinging to the top rail and watching breathlessly the saddling of a bronk inside. But she saw Andy at once and beckoned with a slim, gloved hand. Andy left his horse standing with dropped bridle reins and climbed the fence limberly, settling himself astride the top rail to which she clung.

"You bad, wicked *man!* You told a fib, didn't you? All the boys said so when those poor Pilgreens started home." She shook a finger at him, with a sidelong glance which any man would have found disturbing. "They say no one can believe a word you *say!* I think you're perfectly awful!"

Andy opened his mouth to defend himself, but some of the boys in the corral had spied him and he was given a minute's respite while he answered their helloes. When he turned to the girl, she was looking at the stranger who leaned against the fence near the gate, peering into the corral between poles.

"That's the poor boy you fibbed about," she murmured. "If you had only known what *really* is the matter with him—I think it's the most tragic thing I ever heard of!"

Andy glanced again. "He looks all right to me," he said. "Better than I'd expect, after what happened to him last night."

"Oh, but you haven't heard!" She leaned closer, speaking behind her hand. "That poor boy—he just *tottered* down here as the Pilgreens were driving away—and it's lucky for you he didn't come before they left—that lightning shock gave him *amnesia!*"

Since she apparently expected astonishment, Andy permitted his mouth to sag open.

"Mr. Rapponi and that huge man they call Big Medicine were telling me all about it. They say he doesn't remember *who* he is or where he came from, or *anything*." She looked at Andy sidelong. "Mustn't it be simply dreadful not to know anything about your past?"

"That depends," said Andy, gazing thoughtfully at the unquiet group in the middle of the corral. "It's a heap worse not to know anything about your future, don't you think?"

"Oh, but Big Medicine says the poor boy is just worried *sick* over it. He tried so *hard* to tell them his name,—oh, he's looking this way. I *hope* he didn't hear."

Whether he heard or not, the stranger had turned and was walking slowly toward them. Andy watched him curiously. Barring the unmistakable stiff gait of a saddle-galled man and a slight uncertainty in his movements as if he might still be somewhat dazed from the shock, the fellow seemed little the worse for his experience. He was dressed in gray tweed trousers and coat, pale blue shirt and dark blue tie. In spite of the wrinkles and travel stains, his clothes gave him the look of a city-bred man; the pilgrim type which furnishes so much amusement on the cattle ranges. But he carried his

35

shoulders well and his bare head balanced itself almost haughtily upon a powerful neck. His hair was blond and almost as curly as Pink's, and his eyes were blue and set in shallow sockets, curiously pointed at the corners. They did not, however, look especially dazed or bewildered. They were sophisticated eyes, and though they had an Irish twinkle, they did not invite one to share the joke.

"Howdy," said Andy, in a tone that did not commit him to anything.

"Hello yourself," said the other. "I don't remember seeing you around here before." His eyes went to the girl, which of course was natural. "You don't happen to know who I am, do you? I was afraid you wouldn't. No one around here seems to."

"You—you can't remember who you are, at all?" Myrtle's eyes and her voice were soft with sympathy.

"I could be a Chinaman for all I know. So far as I can tell, I'm nameless." He laughed shortly.

"I think it must be perfectly *thrilling,* not to know your name or anything about your past," said Myrtle, in a tone that jarred on Andy's nerves.

"The present is thrilling enough for me," said the stranger. "I'm not worrying right now about my past." And he laughed in a diffident way as he climbed up beside her.

Andy's black eyebrows came together. He looked at Myrtle and saw her edging along to make room for the fellow. She seemed to have forgotten all about last evening in the bay window at the Rogers ranch. And although he stubbornly held to his place beside her, not once did he turn his face toward her. So far as he was concerned, that particular rail was occupied only by Andy Green.

36

ALL IN THE SAME BOAT

THE CLATTER OF KNIVES AND FORKS ON EIGHTEEN enamel plates, and the clink of eighteen tin spoons stirring coffee in eighteen enamel cups had ceased. The confusion of voices talking and laughing together had drifted outside the mess house. In the words of Cal Emmett, old Patsy had sure spread himself on that dinner. Never had the Happy Family gorged themselves in a more hilarious mood, for girls seldom sat down to eat at the long table. Even the Countess and J. G. himself had come down from the White House, and for once in her life the Countess had refrained from making disparaging remarks about the cooking. Old Patsy's blueberry pies had never been more luscious, and Patsy wore an unaccustomed smile as he began clearing away the debris of the feast.

"Looks like the Meekers aren't coming at all," Weary remarked, halting outside the door to roll a smoke before he settled himself on the tarp which some of the boys had thoughtfully spread in the shade for the girls to sit on while the Happy Family rested for awhile in the blissful lethargy of repletion. "They sure missed a good meal," he added.

"Yeah, how about it, Big Medicine?" Cal wanted to know. "Looks like that new schoolma'am's throwed off on yuh."

"And how about that purty ride you was goin' to make all so fast?" Slim bantered in his slow and heavy drawl. "Way you et, you'll be crawlin' off into the strawpile to snooze with the rest of 'em. Not castin' no reflections on the hogs," he added in ponderous levity.

"If I done that, I'd shore have to root you outa your

nice warm nest," Big Medicine came back at him. "Ever see a human bein' poke so much warm pie into his face as Slim done?" He turned and grinned widely at Myrtle Forsyth who sat next to him, her slim booted feet tucked under her blue riding skirt.

"You sure Joe said he was coming over?" Weary's eyes lifted to scan the trail where it dipped down over the crest of the high bluff and began its winding descent to the creek bottom.

"Shore, he was. Schoolma'am was crazy to see some real bronk ridin', and Joe, he said he'd hitch up and bring the folks awn over. Last thing he said to me was, he'd be here somewheres around noon." Big Medicine canted an eye upward, then sent a sweeping glance around the yard. "Shadders say it's one o'clock or thereabouts."

"If you're talking about the Meekers," Len Adams said, strolling down from the White House arm-in-arm with Rena Jackson, "I saw a rig just coming down that long ridge below their place, as we rode up out of Dry Gulch. They sure ought to be here by now. They weren't more than an hour behind us."

"Well, they might as well not come as to git insulted and have to leave after they git here," growled Happy Jack, with a resentful glance at Andy Green. "Mis' Pilgreen'll have it in fer the hull outfit, from now on. I betcha she won't let a feller near the house after what Andy went and done."

"Me? I never spoke to the old gal, only to pass the time of day," Andy protested virtuously.

"Aw, gwan. I know what she said when I met 'em down the crick. You can't crawl out of it, either."

"But it does seem queer the Meekers haven't come yet," Len Adams tactfully changed the subject. "I know it must have been them I saw coming. You know how

38

Joe drives; there was a streamer of dust for half a mile down that slope. It couldn't have been any one else— they hadn't left the big field yet, so they had to be coming from Meekers'."

"That team's pretty steady," Weary comforted himself. "Still, accidents will happen. Maybe somebody better ride up on the bench and take a look."

"There's a dust up there now," declared Pink, and every face was immediately turned toward the hill road.

"Not enough for a team and wagon," Cal remarked. "Stock hanging around up there, looks like to me."

"Horsebackers," Slim stated heavily, and heads nodded acquiescence while they watched.

"It can't be Joe and the schoolma'am," Len insisted. "That Miss Brumley can't ride off a walk to save her life. She'd be falling off before she reached the gate. I know. I saw her trying to ride Joe's old Kate, and she just hung on for dear life and lost every hairpin out of her head and screamed blue murder because Kate started to trot a little." Her eyes turned involuntarily toward the stranger, who was standing with his back against the log wall, though every other person was sitting. (At least, those sat who were not sprawled lazily upon full stomachs.) Len's brown eyes had an impish gleam, and her teeth showed a white line before she drew her lips together, politely repressing her range-girl's enjoyment of the stranger's predicament, which she thoroughly understood.

"There's five of 'em, anyway," said Weary. "The whole family wouldn't be riding horseback when they've just bought that new double-seated buggy. Now, what does that mean, do you suppose?"

Up on the brow of the hill the five horsemen were halted in earnest conversation. Hands were flung outward in

39

gestures of argument. While those below watched curiously, four of the riders came on down the first steep pitch of the hill, while the fifth dismounted and stationed himself beside the road, sitting down in the shade of a huge boulder where he could observe what went on below. Where the bluff levelled off in a rough terrace extending far up and down the coulee, two riders left the trail, one riding to the left and the other to the right.

The Happy Family looked at one another in silence. Without turning his head, the velvety brown eyes of the Native Son slid sidewise toward the stranger. Pink got up with an ostentatious yawn and stood with his thumb hooked lightly inside his chap belt, and without a word the Native Son rose and sauntered to the corner of the cabin, where he paused and began the leisurely rolling of a cigarette which he did not need, since he had dropped an unlighted one as he got up.

"Why, how funny!" said Rena Jackson in her clear, unthinking treble. "They must be looking for stock or something."

"Yeah," said Cal Emmett, in a peculiar, hushed voice, "I reckon they must be." He glanced at Weary, caught an almost imperceptible signal and rose to his feet.

Within three minutes every man in the group was standing, curiously expectant. Weary waited until the two men left on the trail had ridden down off the Hogback and into the willows along the creek, then he turned to the others.

"I guess maybe I better mosey on down and see what it is they want," he said with elaborate carelessness. "You needn't all come. Just make yourselves comfortable. I'll be right back." He looked at Pink and the Native Son, standing with the stranger between them. As if further exertion was far from their intention, they settled their

40

shoulders against the wall and smoked negligently.

"Say, I guess I'll go along, if it's all the same to you," Big Medicine announced suddenly and started to follow. Weary turned, gave him a keen glance and the two went together down the path.

Conversation at the mess house languished. Myrtle Forsyth went over and stood close to the Native Son, looking up into his face and smiling while she whispered. The Native Son whispered in reply, his dark eyes devouring her.

"No fair, whispering in company," said Len, rising and coming toward them. "We know what you're talking about, anyway."

"Sure, we do," the stranger unexpectedly stated. "You think maybe I'm an escaped convict or something, and that's a posse on my trail. Maybe I am; for all I know I might be Jesse James. I don't *feel* like a criminal, but— Honest, I feel like as if some one had spit on my slate and wiped it off clean. I'm just a nameless guy that had his past knocked off." He looked at them with a rueful twist of his lips into what just missed being a smile. "Chances are, that's my past riding up to the stable right now. Can you blame me for feeling kind of edgy about nudging and whispering in this crowd?" Then he laughed mirthlessly. "Don't worry, folks. I'll take my medicine, whatever it is. Anyway—I might be the missing heir, for all I know. I claim the benefit of the doubt for five minutes."

"That's all right, Nameless," Andy Green's quiet drawl answered him. "Seems like I almost know who you are. I haven't got you placed yet, but it's a cinch I never met yuh in the pen—I've never been in one—"

"Yet," Happy Jack finished sourly. "You will be some day, if yuh don't quit your lyin'."

"Oh, cut out the weeping and wailing, Happy! Annie

41

still loves yuh—she told me so. What I wanted to say was, you girls better run along up to your mothers. There might be language passed back and forth that your maws wouldn't want you to hear. Nameless don't know what he's up against, nor we don't. We'd kind a like to have plenty of talkin' room—you get me?"

"Oh, we get you," Len retorted drily. "And we'll stay and ride herd on your tongues, if you don't mind. If Mr. Man here has done something he can't remember, those fellows will break it a lot more gently if ladies are present. Don't you think we ought to stay, Rena?"

"Why, I wouldn't miss it for worlds," Rena promptly replied.

"I think it's just the most *thrilling* thing I ever heard of in my life!" cried Myrtle, whom Len and Rena had rather pointedly ignored. "It's the most *romantic* adventure a person could possibly have. Just think! This poor boy stands here without the slightest *idea* of what those men will say to him when they come up the path. It's like waiting to hear what the *jury* says—"

"What do you know about juries?" Len cut in. "Don't gush so, Myrt. You're not reading Laura Jean Libby just now." She turned to Andy, who was looking at her attentively, as if after long acquaintance he had just decided that he did not know Len Adams. "I think we may as well stay and see the thing through. There is such a thing as hospitality. Our nameless guest is entitled to our full support, don't you think?" She looked at the stranger with a smile of understanding. "Every man is a gentleman till he proves himself the other thing," she told him. "And there's no use jumping to conclusions. They may not be concerned with you at all. You see, they aren't breaking their necks to get their hands on you."

42

"By gracious, that's right." Andy was staring fixedly down the slope. "That looks like Al Roberts and Mel Davisson, to me. Mel's a deputy sheriff, all right— probably Al is too, for the time being. Why don't they get off their horses, or ride up here, or something? What're they edging off like that for? Come on, boys. Let's drift down that way and see what's the matter. Want to come, Nameless?"

"Sure, I'll come." The pilgrim moved reluctantly away from the wall. With the indefinable look of a hunted animal brought to bay, he glanced toward the brush-fringed creek no more than a pistol shot away. "As Miss Forsyth so cleverly put it, the jury is ready—" He lifted his shoulders in a shrug that accepted his fate and walked stiffly down the path with the others.

"All right for you, Andy Green," called Len. "For half a cent I'd tag along. Shall we, Rena?"

"Oh, let's!"

So the two linked arms as if to push Myrtle Forsyth farther from them, and went down the slope after the boys, loitering in spite of themselves because they knew they were not wanted, but stubbornly proving their independence nevertheless by going. They were nearly to the big gate when they heard one of the horsemen shout.

"You stay where you're at—*all* of yuh! Don't yuh come another step closer! You got your orders, now keep 'em. There'll be men guardin' this coulee on all sides, and they've got orders to shoot anybody that tries to make a break away from here."

"Aw, gwan!" Happy Jack's voice interrupted in raucous protest. "You dassent shoot nobody!"

"You try it once—if yuh feel lucky," the other made ominous retort. "That's the law, and we're here to

43

enforce it. Where's J. G.? It's him I want to serve notice on."

"He's coming," Andy Green announced, glancing back toward the house.

Mystified, the girls drew aside from the path and the Old Man went past them, truculence in every line of his stubby figure. They followed hesitantly, curious to hear what it was all about. So was old J. G. curious, judging from his pace and the way he barked questions.

"Keep back, J. G.," Mel Davisson warned, reining his horse away. "Don't come any closer than what you are. You've got smallpox on the ranch and I'm puttin' you all under quarantine. I want you to see it's kept."

"Smallpox?" The Old Man turned himself slowly about, searching faces until he came to Andy Green, whom he transfixed with a withering stare. "Dawgone you, Andy, I've stood about all I'm goin' to from you. Now you can roll your bed and git off the ranch. A joke's a joke, but I'll be dawgoned—"

"Say, this ain't no joke!" Mel Davisson's voice rose angrily. "We followed that man to where we found his horse—struck by lightnin', accordin' to all the sign—and we saw where a bunch had rode out from this coulee to that horse. Fresh horse tracks, made this mornin'. We saw where they come back again. We've spent a couple hours back up on the bench there, watchin' this place. Meekers we turned back, right up there about a half a mile this side your gate. I sent a man back to town with word for the county health officers—"

"I don't care a dawgone who yuh follered or who yuh sent for!" stormed the Old Man. "There's no dawgoned smallpox on this ranch, and there ain't been. Andy, here—"

"Aw, what's he got to do with it? Don't I know what

44

I'm talkin' about?" He leveled a shaking finger at the pilgrim. "That man and his pardner got off a freight night before last at the water tank. They come into town about supper time and was around the Elkhorn all evening. Other feller was sick, and he kep' gettin' worse, till along after midnight Rusty Brown got kinda worried about 'im and sent for old Doc to come and take a look at 'im. Doc wasn't in no condition to tell much about it, so Rusty put the feller to bed in his back room there till Doc sobered up some. Yesterday when they went to look 'im over, any fool could tell what ailed 'im. He was broke out from his head to his heels— you couldn't put a pin down on 'im—

"This here feller had been stayin' with his pardner, so he musta been about the first one to find out what was the matter. Time we got organized and went lookin' for 'im to take 'im to the pest house, he'd vamoosed. We been huntin' him ever since." He eyed the frozen group, one after the other, and came back to J. G. "You know I hate like h—everything to do it, J. G.—but you know I got to. Old Doc was sober this morning, and he told me it's about as bad a case as he ever saw in his life. He thinks the feller's goin' to die. That there's his pardner, standin' right over there. Even if he ain't come down with it yet, he will b'fore long. And this hull ranch is exposed." He spread his hands in a gesture of ominous finality.

"So that's how she lays. I'm under oath to do my duty and you know what that is. I guess I could trust this bunch—but the law don't take no chances, in a case like this. There'll be more men out from town b'fore night to patrol this coulee. And a doctor'll be down from Benton to vaccinate the hull outfit. Any supplies you want, or any word you want t' send, you can send somebuddy up

45

as far as that white rock up there by the trail. There'll be somebuddy ride down part way from the top to take your message, and stuff'll be delivered that far down. S'long—it's hell, but it can't be helped."

They stood in stunned silence and watched him ride back to join his companion who had remained discreetly in the background probably with a gun handy in case of trouble.

"Hunh!" said the Old Man at last, and turned without a word and left them standing there.

"Boys, I'm damned sorry for this," said the stranger, in a voice that shook perceptibly. "If I'd ever dreamed—"

"Oh, dry up!" snarled Cal Emmett under his breath.

"No, but on the square, I don't see how I could ever have left my partner in a fix like that. I—it ain't *in* me to do a dirty trick like that." He sent an anxious, almost beseeching glance from one to another. "And you must remember I didn't come over here of my own accord. I couldn't have been heading for this place at all. I don't know where I was going, or why, but I must have had some good reason—some errand—It's all a blank. But one thing you've got to admit. I was carried here without my knowledge or consent."

"That," said the Native Son in a tone as smooth as glare ice—and as cold—"that is what I call gratitude!"

"It's the truth," Big Medicine made instant answer. "Nameless wasn't ridin' within eight mile of the ranch. If anybody's to blame for packin' smallpox in here, I am, by cripes!"

"Anybody that blames you has got me to lick, old-timer," said Pink, and slapped Big Medicine on the back.

"Smallpox!" Weary's eyes went meditatively to

46

where the three women stood scared, in the path just beyond the big gate. "Quarantined—oh, mamma!"

"An act of God, *amigo*," the Native Son said softly, and smiled as his brown eyes rested on Myrtle Forsyth.

AND PULLING TOGETHER

"ANDY HAD A RIGHT TO PUT US WISE, SAME AS HE DID the Pilgreens," Bing Adams, phlegmatic brother of Len, complained. "I thought we was good enough friends to get tipped off to a thing like this before the trap was sprung." Bing was a stocky young man who took life and his ranch work seriously. "Smallpox or no smallpox, I'm going home," he said flatly. "I've got to plough up that patch down by the crick to-morrow and cut a sack or two of potato seed. I got no time to be layin' around here." He thrust both hands deep into his pockets and scowled heavily at the two deputies riding up out of the willows beyond the ford.

"Yes, but I was just joshing old lady Pilgreen," Andy explained patiently. "On the dead, I never dreamed it was the truth."

"Darn right yuh never. If yuh had, yuh wouldn't 'a' told it," Happy Jack sneered.

"All you thought of was gettin' Annie off'n the ranch."

"Aw, come off. You musta had some idee it was so, or you never woulda thought of such a thing." Bing spat disgustedly.

"No, you're dead wrong there, Bing. Andy, he don't need no ideas," Cal Emmett broke in. "Andy, he just opens his mouth and lets the words flow."

"Aw, I betcha this is just some josh Andy ribbed up

47

in town," gloomed Happy Jack. "I betcha this is all a frame-up with them guys up there."

Faces were seen to lighten for a moment. It could be so—experience had long ago proved to the Happy Family that Andy was capable of a thing like that. Then the fantastic hope fluttered to earth again like a broken-winged bird.

"Andy didn't have any way of knowing Big Medicine had packed Nameless down here," Bert Rogers suddenly remembered. "Andy hit our place about fifteen minutes ahead of the storm yesterday. No, he couldn't have framed that little speech of Mel's. 'Tain't possible."

"Aw, gwan!" Happy Jack gloomily insisted. "It don't have to be possible. If it's a lie, Andy'd tell it anyway."

While they discussed him thus frankly, Andy lifted one foot across his other knee, bent and drew a match sharply along the sole. He lighted his cigarette with the leisurely care that bespoke an unruffled temper, blew out his match and dropped it to earth, grinding the stub under his heel.

"Any of you fellows want to take a chance on riding up that trail?" he asked carelessly, after his second mouthful of smoke. "Go on, Happy. You try it."

"Aw, I don't haff to. All us boys has done ever since you come here is ride around provin' you're a—josher." The last word was so evidently a hasty revision that every one laughed.

"No use beefing around about it, boys," Weary interrupted the argument. "As the Countess says, 'Man plans and God displans.' We're up against it right, if you ask me. What we've got to do is make our plans. Here's Nameless, been scatterin' germs like a farmer scatters corn for the chickens. We better do something about that."

48

"Yeah. You stand over there, Nameless." Slim suddenly awoke to the perils of infection. "By golly, I don't want no more germs off'n you blowin' onto me."

Audible chuckles greeted that precaution, but there was a noticeable shifting of positions to the windward of the pilgrim. Into the midst of their anxious discussion of the problem the feminine element suddenly projected itself, as so often happens.

"Isn't it *thrilling!*" Len Adams called ironically from beyond the big gate, forestalling Myrtle, whose red lips had opened for some such exclamation. "I think it's just too romantic for words! Have any of you boys broken out yet?"

Heads turned for brief and startled glances.

"You girls had better go on up to the house," Weary advised in the persuasive tone one uses to meddlesome children.

"Will you please tell me why you're always trying to drive us up to the house?" Len demanded with spirit. "I thought misery loved company. Aren't we all in the same boat?"

"Yeah, but you're rockin' it," Pink flung back, his dimples softening the charge.

"We believe in women's rights." Len stood her ground, just inside the big gate. "If that's a council of war you're having, we're going to be in it. Aren't we, Rena?"

"What you can notice," Rena Jackson promptly supported her.

"All right, stay then," Weary called, grinning queerly. "We kinda thought we better do this job alone. Come on, Nameless."

"Oh, what are you going to *do* to him?" shrieked Myrtle, running toward them. "Will Davidson, you

49

leave that poor boy alone. Every one knows it isn't his fault—when he was carried here unconscious and couldn't *help* himself. You leave him *alone,* I tell you!" For the first time that day, Myrtle Forsyth showed symptoms of real emotion. "He isn't to blame," she reiterated, tears standing in her narrow blue eyes.

"No, he's more to be pitied than censured," the Native Son agreed, taking a step toward Myrtle.

"I won't have him abused by that brute of a Will Davidson! He's capable of *anything!*" Myrtle's voice held more than a hint of tears.

"Oh, go on up to the house, Myrt," her cousin Bert commanded, quite unimpressed. "Don't start bawling."

"But what *are* you boys going to do with him?" With a broken engagement lying unmended between Bert Rogers and herself, Len Adams' tone was brusque. "Myrt's absolutely right, for once in her life. He isn't to blame for being here."

"Smallpox don't stop to ask who's to blame," Bert Rogers retorted.

"No, by golly, it don't," cried Slim. "Us fellers has got to pertect ourselves, regardless of who's to blame."

"But what are you going to do?" Len advanced purposefully through the gate. "We'll stick worse than sand burrs till you tell us exactly what you boys are going to do to him."

The Happy Family looked at one another in some embarrassment. Then Weary threw up his hands in a gesture of exasperation, though his lips twitched.

"Well, if you must know, we're going to take Nameless down to the creek and strip him, and put him to soak while we burn the clothes he's wearing. You sand burrs can stick as tight as yuh darn please. Come along, Nameless."

"You better soak your heads while you're about it," Len made angry retort, though her face turned crimson from collar to hat brim. "You're liable to get brain fever, you're so smart all at once. Come on, Rena."

Their haughty retreat, somewhat marred by surreptitious giggling, was watched in dead silence by the Happy Family, until the girls reached the steps of the White House porch. Then Weary's gaze returned to the stranger. He crooked a beckoning finger.

"Say, why don't you wise birds get busy and do a little thinking?" Nameless protested while they closed in on him, shooing him toward the bunk-house. "If you burn my clothes, somebody will have to donate another suit." He added with extreme irony. "Didn't you guys ever hear of such a thing as fumigation?"

"Keep moving," Weary ordered grimly, and canted an inquiring look toward the others.

"All I've got in the world, so far as I know, is this suit of clothes and that little satchel you say is mine. I can't see the point in burning them, when disinfection will answer the same purpose and I won't have to be beholden to you guys for the clothes on my back. All this scare about smallpox is just so much poppycock, if you ask me—"

"How do you know?" the Native Son caught him up. "I thought you couldn't remember anything."

"I can't. But a fellow can have a hunch, can't he? That wise bird on the horse didn't sound convincing to me, somehow. But I'm willing to play the game—"

"Hell," snorted Pink, "nobody asked you to be willing."

"It might make it simpler for you guys if I am. I'll take a bath—"

"Darn right, you will."

51

"But I'll be damned if I'll stand for having my clothes burnt."

"No? Just what was you aimin' to do about it?"

"Do? I'll slip up on you when you're asleep and blow my breath on every blamed one of you. I'll—"

"You get in there and get that satchel of yours, and all the beddin' you slept on last night, and bring 'em out here pronto," Weary cut in sternly. "What you'll do don't interest nobody. It's what we'll do that counts around this ranch." But when the stranger sullenly disappeared within the bunk-house, Weary looked at his companions and grinned. "Got spunk, anyway," he remarked. "I wondered about that. Up till right now he's been altogether too flannel-mouthed to suit me."

"There's a bag of sulphur down in the chicken house," Slim said thoughtfully. "I been aimin' to get after them mites, soon as I could git around to it. What say we kill two birds with one stone?"

"If you smoked that *hombre* along with his clothes, you'd be doing a good deed," said the Native Son.

"Sulphur smoke'll kill a human," Slim objected in perfect sincerity.

"I was thinking of that," Miguel replied in his silkiest tone.

This drew fire from Big Medicine, who was sensitive concerning his protégé. Others took a hand in the argument, Andy Green and Pink siding with Big Medicine. The wrangle had only one tangible result, however. It established once and for all the fact that no one had more clothes than he needed for himself. The Happy Family unanimously decided to fumigate Nameless along with the chicken mites, and let it go at that.

So they herded him and his load to the henhouse

52

which was roomy and fairly clean. They drove him, swearing, inside to disrobe, and they crowded doorway and window to watch the proceeding and to offer ribald comment and advice. Even Big Medicine and the Native Son forgot their incipient feud and chortled together when a white hen unexpectedly flew off a nest in an obscure corner and dashed blindly against the muscular bare legs of Nameless, who was at that moment draping his underwear across a roost. Followed fluent blasphemy and a hysterical cackling, while the Happy Family blocked all exits and roared.

"By this and by that I'll get even for this, and I'll get even right!" gasped Nameless, when the tumult subsided and he was standing sweating and breathless, the white hen, plaintively squawking, clasped tight to his heaving chest. "What I won't do to you! My memory of the past may be gone, but it sure will be working from now on. If it takes ten years—"

"Haw-haw-haw-w-w!" bellowed Big Medicine, tears rolling down his weathered cheeks. And "Hoo-hoo-hoo-oo!" came the cachinnations of the rest.

"I hope you all have smallpox till you look like a mess of tripe," snarled Nameless, a sinister glitter in his eyes. "You laughing hyenas'll sweat blood for this— you mark what I tell you."

"Say, it'll be worth it, by golly," declared Slim huskily, having laughed himself hoarse. "Drag that there tub over into the middle where it won't ketch your things afire. There's paper an' kindlin' all ready in it . . . Now set that there bag of sulphur on it."

"Well, take this damn' chicken, some of you," snapped Nameless, and flung the hen viciously into the face of the Native Son. "It's your turn now, but mine will come. And don't forget that."

53

"All right, Nameless, but in the meantime there's a bath coming your way. Get busy and light your fire." Weary flipped a match inside. Nameless caught it deftly, lighted the fire and leaped naked into their midst. The Happy Family backed hastily, and Slim slammed the door shut and hung an old canvas over it as he always did when waging a periodical war on mites.

"Hand me a blanket, somebody," Nameless implored, craning toward the White House.

"Head for the creek," Weary told him. "We'll walk behind so you won't be seen." Which they proceeded to do, grinning heartlessly while the pilgrim went nipping painfully over the rocks ten feet in advance of them.

However warm may be the sunshine, running water is cold in the month of April in Montana. But the Happy Family could not be bothered with that trivial circumstance. With threats and flipped pebbles they drove the pilgrim shivering into a pool where the water came to his middle, and roosted in a row on the bank to see that he was thorough.

"Souse down into it, Nameless! It'll feel warmer after awhile."

"Sure! Nothin' like gittin' used to a thing," Bing Adams encouraged.

"Say, here's the carbolic. It ain't strong—been setting on a shelf for a year and lost darn near all its strength," said Pink. "Sprinkle it onto your head good. Germs stick in the hair something terrible."

Nameless foolishly obeyed, gave an abrupt howl and submerged himself completely while the Happy Family writhed in convulsions of mirth on the bank. He came up blue and chattering and they let him out on dry land. Big Medicine went off and gleaned a horse blanket from the shed, wrapped the pilgrim solicitously, and led him

54

to the nearest haystack where he might sit in the sun and wait for his clothes.

"How long?" he controlled the tremble of his chin to ask with ominous calm.

"Till the sulphur's all burnt up and the smoke quits pourin' out the cracks," Slim informed him. "Mites is hard to kill and so is germs, by golly. You got to give 'em both plenty uh time."

"You might stake me to a cigarette, somebody."

"Smoke in that haystack? Not on your life!" Weary denied him the indulgence in a shocked tone. "Come on, boys. We've got to set on Big Medicine's case next. Packing Nameless clear over from Dry Gulch the way he did—Mamma, I bet he's plumb polluted with germs!"

"Darn right," several voices made instant agreement. "Gosh, why didn't we think of that before? We coulda smoked him same time we did Nameless."

"You go to granny," said Big Medicine. "I had my slicker on and it was pourin' rain. Any germs that lit on me was washed off into the road. What about Mig, over there? He packed that satchel home behind his cantle; and all the rest of yuh that undressed that pore feller last night and dried his clothes for 'im? Looks to me like you're all tarred with the same stick, by cripes."

The Happy Family looked at him dubiously.

"By golly, that's right," Slim admitted. "We'd oughta saved out some of that sulphur for the bunk-house. What'd yuh do with that there carbolic, Pink? I'm goin' to wash my clothes."

While enough sulphur smoldered in the henhouse to fumigate every building on the ranch, the Happy Family toiled with strong lye water and carbolic acid, sterilizing the bunk-house and that portion of the mess house

55

which Nameless had occupied. Blankets flapped on barbed-wire fences, and the bushes down by the creek flowered with laundry washed to the tune of loud and acrimonious argument.

They nearly forgot Nameless, wrapped in the horse blanket and vengeful meditations beside the haystack. When he came slipping up to the bunk-house at dusk they had no heart for banter. They were watching the distant flicker of flame up on the brow of the hill where their guards were cooking supper, and they were thinking uneasily that, take what measures they might, this quarantine business was going to be no joke.

PEACE IS THE WORD

MONDAY PASSED SO QUIETLY THAT THE OLD MAN began again to cast distrustful glances toward Andy Green. The Happy Family rode bronks they had expected to ride the day before, with the girls looking on from the vantage point of the hay-rack. Nameless had recovered his clothes and with them his temper, and was tacitly accepted as an unexpected guest who seemed pleasant enough and quite inoffensive for a city guy, even if he did beat it out of town and leave his partner sick with smallpox. Big Medicine argued that the pore feller probably didn't realize that he was taking the disease along with him, and for all anybody knew he might have had some important mission in the Badlands or wherever he was headed for. Until they knew the straight of it, they ought to let that subject drop; which they did.

For one thing, Tuesday gave them something new to think about. Tuesday brought a doctor from Fort

56

Benton, armed with vaccine enough for the whole Bear Paw country. The Happy Family bared arms cheerfully enough and guyed one another about growing horns and hoofs, as the doctor—a jolly old fellow—told them was once believed to be the result of vaccinating with cowpox. They pretended to accept the old superstition as a scientific fact, but underneath their banter they were visibly impressed with the gravity of the situation.

Even Happy Jack had to admit that this did not look like one of Andy Green's tricks. Wholesale vaccination by a doctor from the county seat meant business, however much he might joke about it. Nothing to be afraid of, though. Sore arms for a day or so when the stuff began to take hold, and after that they could forget about it. Just a safety law that would hold them in the coulee for twelve days,—unless Nameless came down with smallpox, of course. In that case, the quarantine would have to be extended.

The doctor examined Nameless and pronounced him in splendid physical condition. As to the loss of memory, that of course was the result of the lightning shock and probably would right itself in time. There was nothing he could do about it, he said. Time, plenty of exercise in the open air, normal conditions of living— really, the life he was living here on the ranch was what any physician would prescribe for him. The doctor was interested, but not especially concerned. The man's partner in Dry Lake was delirious, he said, and there was no information to be gained there. Confluent smallpox was a serious matter, and the proper treatment had been lacking at the beginning of the case. He was a very sick man. It was doubtful whether he would recover.

He did not stay longer than was necessary, because he

meant to vaccinate every man, woman and child in the district as a precautionary measure. With proper vaccination, he assured them in leaving, the danger of an epidemic was greatly minimized; and if they did contract the disease, it was not likely to prove fatal.

With those cheering words he walked down to the willows at the ford, where a livery rig from town and the means of disinfecting himself had waited. And for the rest of the week the Happy Family worked with their bronks and made a game of it, the girls usually looking on.

Sunday morning came again, warm as June and with a brooding stillness broken only by the cheerful cackling of hens in the miteless chicken house. Down by the creek, Andy Green sat with his back against a rock shaded by a young cottonwood tree, and listlessly carved an intricate pattern of serpentine stripes down a green willow stick which he was painstakingly fashioning into a cane for Len Adams. Twice in the last three minutes he had paused in his work to feel with gentle finger tips a certain place on his swollen left bicep, midway between elbow and shoulder. He had laid down the stick and was unbuttoning his shirtsleeve for a closer inspection when Pink came along, a bundle of soiled socks and handkerchiefs wadded into the crook of one arm.

"Oh, hello, Andy," he gave casual greeting. "How's she coming?"

"Sore as seventeen boils. She's swellin' like a poisoned pup. I been sick as a dog ever since last night, but I can't lay and listen to Happy. How's yours?"

Pink immediately hunkered down on his boot-heels, dropped his laundry and unbuttoned his own left sleeve.

"She's slow," he said, "but oh, man, she's sure. I

58

thought I'd get my washing done before it gets any worse. Say, Slim's arm's like a stovepipe this morning. You see it?" He leaned to look as Andy's sleeve went slowly up. "Boy, you're sure going to have a pippin," he passed critical judgment. "Cal's laid out, did you know that?"

"By gracious, I'd about as soon have smallpox and be done with it." Andy drew slow fingers across his aching eyes. "Nameless ain't showing any signs of coming down yet, is he?"

"Him?" Pink rolled up the other sleeve, gathered up his washing and went to squat beside the creek. "Nothing fazes that guy. He's gone for a walk with Myrt. First thing he knows, he'll think he's tangled with a mess of wildcats. Native Son won't stand for him walkin' Myrt around, I tell yuh those." He pulled a worn cake of soap from his hip pocket, pushed back his big hat, trailed a blue dotted handkerchief in the water, lifted it dripping and began soaping it vigorously.

"You oughtn't to dabble in that cold water, Pink. Countess says you're liable to die if yuh catch cold in that arm," Andy gave perfunctory warning.

"Yeah, I know she does. Say, what do you think? Is Mig serious about that red *loco* gal, or is he just playin' up to her for the fun of it?"

"Search me. You can't tell what's goin' on back of them romantic eyes of his. He sure acts like he's building his loop for Myrt, all right." Andy whittled without interest.

"From what the boys that knows her tell me, any man is sure ridin' for a fall that takes Myrt serious. You heard about her and Weary, didn't yuh?"

"Yeah, I heard. Len was telling me the other day."

"I s'pose yuh know Bert's crazy about Len," Pink

59

glanced over his shoulder to say constrainedly.

"Yeah, I know it. It might help some if Bert let her know it too. Len's a good kid. Straight as they grow, but proud as the devil. Bert's a fool, that's all I got to say."

"Nameless seems to be kinda makin' himself the white-haired boy with Len too," Pink observed in a relieved tone. "He'll run into Bert if he don't look out. And I caught a look in Bing's eyes when Nameless was whisperin' something to Rena. Nameless is buildin' himself all kinds of trouble, if you ask me." He rinsed and wrung the blue handkerchief, spread it upon a warm, flat rock and reached for a pair of socks small enough for a woman's feet.

Andy cupped his right palm beneath his left elbow and moved that arm to a new position, wincing at the pain. He drew his hand again across his forehead.

"Gosh, but I feel tough!" he sighed. "Would you mind bringing me a blanket and a pillow down here, Pink? I'd rather lay out here than in that darn bunkhouse."

"Yeah, I don't blame you. Them that's up are crabbing over a card game up there. Sore as she-bears, the whole bunch of 'em. It sure ain't any place to carry a headache into." Pink stood wiping his hands while he surveyed the sick man. Andy had slumped down upon his shoulder blades and his head dropped upon his chest. "Anything I can bring you? Coffee or something? You didn't eat any breakfast."

But Andy did not want any coffee. When he opened his eyes, the treetop above him seemed to sway drunkenly, though there was no wind. His left arm felt like a dry log in flames. By the time Pink returned, Andy considered himself the sickest man in the outfit.

"Weary says you got to go crawl into bed," Pink

announced. "It's pretty quiet up there right now. Big Medicine and Mig had another run-in over Nameless, but Weary calmed 'em down before they got past the talkin' stage. Their arms are too sore to fight, anyway. You better go on up, Andy. Weary thinks you're liable to catch cold down here."

"Oh, hell!" Andy muttered, but he got up obediently. Weary was boss of the bunk-house while Chip was away, and what he said might as well be considered law.

In the bunk-house the card game had been abandoned, matches and white beans heaped promiscuously in the center of the table just as they had been pushed there by the disgruntled players. Happy Jack was standing before the broken mirror, distressfully searching his flushed countenance. The sight of him cheered Andy immensely. He managed a sickly grin as he walked over and with his well hand pulled Happy's collar loose at the back.

"Gwan away f'm me," Happy Jack said crossly. "You fellers are just plain damn' liars. I ain't broke out at all."

"Let's have another look, Happy. The back of the neck is where they show up first in red-headed folks." Andy plucked and peered again. "What's that spot down there between your shoulders? Don't it feel sore or anything?"

"Aw, gwan away. You're just lyin'." Happy twitched himself free, but his well arm went up, fingers groping at his back.

The Happy Family laughed at that, and Andy advised him not to be a chump and believe everything he was told. "You know darn well, Happy, another week almost will have to go by before any of us could come down. You heard what that doctor told us; twelve days.

61

Nameless is different. Nobody's got a line on Nameless—yet."

His gray eyes, somewhat glassy now with the fever burning within him, turned for a glance at the pilgrim. Nameless was down on one knee beside his bunk, looking for his little black satchel. He drew back his hand, resting his finger tips on the floor while he looked up at Andy. The posture reminded Andy of something. He shut his eyes and stood scowling, pain and an illusive memory racking him.

"Meaning what?" The pilgrim still crouched, eyeing him between half-closed lids.

"Oh, nothing, I guess. Gosh, but I feel rocky!"

Andy walked listlessly over to his bed and lay down, nursing his arm, and for the rest of that day never once opened his lips. Pain was still warring with memory, and strange distorted pictures came, held him absorbed for a while, then blurred and left him. Voices mumbled, rose in petulant dispute, subsided to uneasy silence in the bunk-house. He heard some one slam the door and say the Old Man wanted somebody to ride up and hail a guard and send word into town for a doctor. Old Jim Jackson, father of Rena, was plumb out of his head, and they needed help at the White House. He heard Big Medicine's loud voice volunteering to go, and he was troubled by something in the tone the Native Son used in adding his own offer.

"By cripes, they want *white* help up there!" Big Medicine shouted in his rough bellow, and there was the sudden scuffing of feet on the bare floor.

Andy opened his eyes, tried to sit up. Nausea seized him and he lay down again with a groan. That darned fool of a Big Medicine—did he want to get himself knifed? Then Weary's calm authoritative voice cut through the ominous silence like a clean wind parting a fog bank.

"Jar loose, you fellows. If I thought Big Medicine was responsible right now, I'd take a whack at him myself, Mig. He ain't, though. He's just talking to hear his head roar. Nameless, you're teacher's pet right now; you go on and set up with the sick. Maybe you can get by without tangling. Go on—beat it. J. G.'s up there alone with the women, and old Jackson's crazy as a loon. You'll have plenty to do, holding him in bed. And it serves you right," he added banteringly, as the door opened and closed again.

"Now, Mig, you go to bed and try and get some sleep," Weary continued persuasively. "You'll forget all about it by morning."

"Me? I never forget. First it is greaser, and now—"

"You know Big Medicine. He's like a she-bear with one lone cub. You called Nameless a crook, right after Big Medicine saved his life. Do you think for a minute he's going to admit he got off wrong? Here's this smallpox scare, right on top of all our joshing, and Big Medicine's touchy as the very devil about it. He knows darned well he's the one that's responsible for all this trouble, and yet it was that big heart of his that let us in for it. He wouldn't have had it happen for the world. He may try to bluff it out, but I know it's got Big Medicine where he lives. He don't see how he could have done any different, though, and I don't either. If you or I or any of the rest of us had ridden along there when he did, we'd have packed that pilgrim to the ranch, same as Big Medicine did."

"We wouldn't insult—"

"Oh, I don't know," drawled Weary. "I guess we'd try and justify our deed of kindness. We'd hate like sin to own up we'd made a mistake."

63

Andy lifted his heavy lids and saw Weary standing just inside the door, both hands on Miguel's shoulders while he talked.

"As for you—I can't see why 'greaser's' any worse than 'bog-trotter,' and that's what Big Medicine called me yesterday. That's just his way—lamming a fellow on any spot he thinks is sore. It don't mean a thing in the world, Mig, and you know it. You don't want to pay any attention—"

"No," chimed in Pink. "Just consider the source, as the fellow said when the mule—"

"Aw, chestnuts!" Happy Jack's raucous protest interrupted him. "Can't yuh think up something new?"

"By gracious, I'll insult the bunch of you if you don't saw off," Andy suddenly threatened. "You take that honor of yours and wrap it in cotton, Mig, and lay it away till this war's over. I've got a headache."

"Yeah, I been insulted too," Cal Emmett spoke up. "I didn't go up in the air about it, though. I was joshing Nameless about his loss of memory and Big Medicine—"

"I guess we could all dig up something to build a grudge around if we wanted to," Weary cut in. "We've got to step careful around them two. Nameless is a maverick and we don't know where he stands or what he might be capable of. He's got me guessing, I'll admit that much. Big Medicine we know. He's got a heart like an ox—"

"And a head like a bull, same as his voice," came from Pink.

"Mule, you mean," Andy muttered the amendment.

"Well, he's a mixture of both, maybe," Weary conceded equably. "The point is, he's so darned touchy about Nameless we better all of us ride 'way around that subject when he's in hearing. We're going to be close-

64

herded on this ranch for Lord knows how long. It would be the dickens of a note if we got to quarreling amongst ourselves. If we can't keep peace in the family—"

"Oh, all right," the Native Son yielded grudgingly. "Peace is the word, *amigo*. But I say to you now, that Nameless one is not fooling me with his lost memory. I don't like him—"

"You don't have to like him. All you have to do is keep it to yourself."

"—and Big Medicine cannot push me too far. Talk of peace to him, *amigo*."

"Don't think I won't," Weary answered, a tired look in his eyes as his hands dropped from Miguel's shoulders. "Better turn in, Mig. We'll all feel better tomorrow, maybe."

There was sense in what he said. Soon a somnolent silence settled upon the bunk-house, and if it were not peace it at least answered that purpose for a time. But Weary lay long awake that night, and behind Andy Green's closed eyelids strange thoughts and half-waking visions came and went.

VICTIM NUMBER ONE

"BY GRACIOUS!" ANDY YAWNED, WITH THE SUN shining full in his eyes one morning. "I've heard of a month of Sundays, but I never saw it happen before. Not right in the time when spring round-up oughta be starting." He lay knuckling his eyes with his well hand, the other arm being still too sore for unguarded movement. Over in the far corner of the bunkhouse Slim's bed creaked as he shifted his heavy bulk, and across the narrow space between bunks Pink's curly blond head burrowed deeper into the pillow. Some one went *"Ee-ee-ow"* (as nearly as such a sound can be spelled), yawning luxuriously; but no one made a move to get up and dress.

"Hello the house!" called Andy, after a minute, and leaned to fumble in his pants pocket for his watch. "You all petrified, or what? Gosh, it's past seven!" This, you must know, was a disgraceful hour for the Happy Family to be rising on a bright morning in spring. "Crawl out, worms. The early bird has flew to roost."

"Aw, can that noise," some one advised. It sounded like Happy Jack's voice. "Patsy ain't called breakfast yet."

"He's probably out flaggin' our guard to come down and bury this bunch, thinkin' we're dead." Andy sat up, ran his fingers through his brown hair and swung limberly out of bed. His glance wandered around the room and rested upon tumbled blankets on the bed next to Pink's.

"Shame on you lazy hounds! Here's the pilgrim, up hours ago. Hey, Mig! Better come alive, there. Nameless is out browsing around the red *loco* patch already."

"Say, what business is that of Mig's?" Big Medicine heaved himself up in his bed to demand truculently.

"Hey, who wants to ride that ginger-colored bronk to-day?" Andy reached mechanically for his hat, set it on his head and proceeded to pull on his boots awkwardly, with grunts and grimaces making it plain to his world that he still suffered partial disablement.

Pink sat up and in a whisper began counting on his fingers.

"—Nine—ten—this is Tuesday, ain't it?— Wednesday—Thur—two more days, boys, and they've

66

got to let us out. I guess we're all safe from catchin' anything." His gaze rested meditatively on the empty bunk where the pilgrim had slept. "And that doctor said twelve days is the limit. Looks like we're pretty safe. Roll out, you fellows!"

"We oughta be able to start on round-up in a week, anyway," said Weary. "And Bing can go home and plant his spuds. Poke your heads out here, boys, and let's have a look at you. Yep—you're a hard-lookin' bunch of rannies, all right, but you don't show any spots, thank the Lord." He went to the door, opened it and glanced out. "There comes Nameless, trotting up the trail like a grey wolf. He's an ambitious cuss, I'll say that for him."

"Yeah, he makes the rounds of the coulee every morning," Big Medicine stated proudly. "On the high lope too, by cripes. He—"

"*Afoot?*"

"Yeah, afoot." Big Medicine went and stood in the doorway, looking over Weary's shoulder. "Ever see a man trot along any more graceful than that?" He pointed an unnecessary finger. "Lookit! Took that gate like a deer! By cripes, he's goin' t' do it again! You watch 'im now."

The Happy Family converged swiftly upon the doorway and window. Down by the big gate the pilgrim was dragging a foot across the road, marking a line in the dust. On the fence two panels away, a bronze hen turkey stood craning and *querk-querking* uneasily, while on the ground a great gobbler strutted. The boom of his vibrating wing feathers came plainly to the ears of the Happy Family while the pilgrim stood poised upon the score mark he had made.

"By golly, lookit that, would yuh!" Slim elbowed his

67

neighbor excitedly. "Went over that gate light as a feather!"

"And there ain't a man awn the ranch could equal that jump awn horseback!" boasted Big Medicine. "Now he's comin' back over this side. Take a look at that there, by cripes!"

Five clean jumps the pilgrim made, the Happy Family watching him in wordless amazement.

"Aw, I knowed he was some relation to a flea," Happy Jack grunted disparagingly, when the pilgrim made his sixth leap and landed on all fours like a cat.

"The jumping son-of-a-gun!" Pink exclaimed admiringly. "Oh, look! *Look,* boys! Wow-ow!"

No one had taken notice of the bronze gobbler's increasing emotion. His violent gobbling as he strutted and drummed was too familiar a sound for the senses to register. Now he hurled himself full on the pilgrim's bowed back, beating him unmercifully over the head with one wing, over the haunches with the other and raking the pilgrim's back with his two-inch spurs. One cannot ignore a twenty-pound turkey gobbler on the warpath. Nameless flattened beneath the weight of him and yelled, his face in the dust, arms flailing and clutching ineffectively.

"Lemme outa here! I'll shoot the damn' thing," shouted Big Medicine, struggling against the human barricade in the doorway. It was Weary who clutched him and hauled him back.

"You stay where you're at. Nameless 'll likely kill yuh if you go butting in right now. If that guy can't protect himself from a *turkey*—"

"Shore he can!" Big Medicine saw the point. "Mrs. Chip 'll have to get her another gobbler, that's all. Time Nameless gits through with 'im—"

"Nameless is through right now," shrilled Pink, "only old Chief don't know it! Yee-*oww!* Ride 'im, gobbler! Rake 'im from ears to flank! That's the stuff!"

At the risk of losing an eye, Nameless rolled and clutched the great bird. Dust rose in spurts where he writhed and wrestled. The Happy Family swarmed out and raced to the scene of battle, shouting encouragement; though whether it was meant for Nameless or the turkey was not made clear.

The pilgrim struggled somehow to his feet and old Chief dropped to the ground. But even then the fight was not over. Feathers flew. Every chicken within gunshot set up a terrific cackling as the gobbler leaped and nipped viciously, dodging the pilgrim's kicks and blows until exhaustion weakened the attack. As the pilgrim fought his way slowly up the trail, he spied a piece of neck-yoke and somehow managed to duck and grab it. Old Chief, having a thorough understanding of sticks, retreated down the slope, gobbling defiance and dragging broken wing feathers as he went.

"That darn bird fouled me!" laughed Nameless, ruefully inspecting his tattered shirt. "Some scrapper!"

"You or old Chief?" Cal wanted to know between spasms. "Brother, that bird sure rode yuh straight up for a few jumps."

"Speaking of jumps," said Weary, when the laughter had subsided, "what was you trying to do down there before the turkey bought into the game?"

Nameless flushed a little. "Oh—I kind of like to get out and ramble, every morning," he grinned sheepishly. "I discovered that a good run gives me an appetite for breakfast. I like to circle the ranch and see what the guards are doing—and say, boy, they sure do back up when I start towards them! One up the coulee almost took a shot at me this morning. He would, I guess, if I hadn't turned back. Then—oh, that jumping? Well, the gate was shut when I came along and I had a sudden notion to jump it. It was easier than I expected. I just kept on jumping for the fun of it—till that darned turkey got a half Nelson on me—"

"Say, what the deuce do you know about half Nelsons?" Bert Rogers caught him up.

"Hunh?" the pilgrim looked blank. "I don't know anything about it, I guess. It's just a slang phrase, isn't it?" He looked at the Happy Family questioningly. "I must seem like an awful chump," he apologized. "I say things that I don't know the meaning of after the words are out. I thought maybe if I exercised a lot in the open air, I'd get things straightened out in my head quicker. Honest, I was just tickled to death to find out I could jump that blamed gate. I don't know why, though. I reckon any of you boys can do it."

"Ain't a man awn the ranch can do what you done," Big Medicine asserted boldly, and sent a challenging glance around him.

"You think so?" The Native Son started abruptly running down the path, lifted himself into the air, and went over the gate in a flying leap and ran on to the stable, a gratifying chorus of cheers sounding behind him.

He should have left it at that. Instead, back he came to repeat the triumph. It was an uphill jump and he was a bit winded. One boot-heel caught and he came down in an ignominious sprawl.

"Haw-haw-*haw-w-w!*" chortled Big Medicine, as the Native Son picked himself up and dodged the irate gobbler which was making for him with blood in his eye. "Yuh will, ay? Thought it was easy, didn't yuh? Haw-haw-*haw-w-w!*"

"You don't want to try that in high-heel boots, Mig," the pilgrim warned him sympathetically. "You'd have made it all right, only for that."

"Yuh don't wanta try that in nothin'," Big Medicine rubbed it in. "You couldn't jump that gate awn horseback, even! Nameless, here, he's—"

The Native Son spoke a long crackling sentence which gave the full rating of Nameless, but fortunately he spoke in Spanish. Then Weary, scenting imminent trouble, sauntered between the two.

"Good shot, Mig. We'll put on our shoes and all have a whirl at it after breakfast. Wonder you didn't break your neck, in those heels. Come on, boys—we ain't washed yet and old Patsy'll be calling breakfast in a minute."

"He better!" Pink supplied further distraction, leading the way to the creek where morning ablutions were usually performed in warm weather. "Come on, Mig. You're so frisky, I'll race yuh to breakfast."

The Native Son's brow cleared a little as he ran after Pink. But Weary, hanging back with the excuse of a cigarette gone cold, made an imperceptible sign to Andy Green, who promptly halted and offered Weary a match.

"For gosh sake, Andy, what are we going to do with them two?" Weary sent a worried glance after the others.

"Let 'em tear into each other and be done with it," Andy retorted. "You can't nurse 'em along only so far. They'll lock horns the minute your back is turned, in spite of hell."

"You know Big Medicine's record," Weary demurred, as the two walked slowly toward the creek. "Best-hearted in the world, till he's stirred past a certain point. Miguel's the same, only he's smoother on the surface. I wish you'd kinda keep an eye out."

71

Andy promised that he would.

"Soon as this quarantine lets up and we get out on round-up, things will straighten out all right," Weary went on. "Nameless will pull out for somewhere and Big Medicine 'll settle down."

"It ain't him so much now, Weary. It's that red-headed cousin of Bert's," Andy told him. "You've been side-stepping the girls, kinda, so you don't see all that goes on. Big Medicine's gone plumb *loco* over Myrt."

"Him? You're crazy. With a face like his—"

"That don't make any difference, Weary. Did you ever see a homely guy that didn't think he was a helluva feller with the ladies? Big Medicine's got it bad. She eggs him on, I'll say that for him. You know how she looks at yuh outa the corner of her eyes?"

"I used to know. I've forgot, thank the Lord."

"There's guys on this ranch that'll wish they could forget. She turns them eyes on Big Medicine. And Mig. And—"

"Mamma!" Weary stopped to grind his cigarette stub under his heel in the path. "If they'd just lead Myrt outa this coulee, we could get along fine with the smallpox."

"That's what," Andy gave emphatic assent. "I'm free to admit Myrt had me going, right at first. All in the world that saved me was seeing her scatter them looks around so promiscuous. That cooked me right then and there."

Weary did not reply. Patsy had yanked open the door of the mess house and was banging a tin pan viciously with a long-handled spoon, and the two took longer steps toward the creek. There the competition on towels was running high. The Native Son and Pink flung one toward Weary and raced off to the mess house, Bert Rogers, Slim and Bing Adams crowding their heels. The

72

others went trooping in after them and straddled the long benches eagerly.

With the odor of fried ham and eggs hanging heavy in the warm air of the long low room, nothing short of actual murder could have dampened the spirits of the Happy Family just then. Now that food was spread before them appetites were ravenous. For the moment, the chief concern of every man there at the table seemed to be the filling of his plate and his stomach. Breakfast was late, but no one mentioned the delinquency now that it was being remedied.

The meal might have proceeded to the end in perfect peace and enjoyment, had not old Patsy inadvertently poured scalding coffee on Cal Emmett's hand instead of into the cup Cal was holding up for a second filling. Cal jumped, swore a customary oath and turned to stare reproachfully at Patsy. Suddenly his round blue eyes widened with horror. He shied violently against his neighbor, who happened to be Slim, and with a howl of dismay scrambled backward over the bench.

"Git away from me!" he shouted, dodging Patsy in his dash to the door.

"Here! What's your hurry?" called Bert.

"Look at 'im!" Cal whirled in the doorway and made a stabbing gesture with his finger. "Old Patsy! *Look* at 'im!"

The Happy Family looked and stampeded for the door. Outside, they stood eyeing the mess house like chickens shut out from their roosts at sundown.

"And I et two biscuits," Happy Jack stated lugubriously and moved aside as Patsy pulled open the door they had slammed upon their departure.

"Vot you poys make now alreatty?" he demanded queruously. "Don't my cooking be goot enough dis morning?"

The Happy Family flapped detaining hands at him and backed away.

"Keep off," warned Cal. "You've got it!"

"I got nottings, py cosh, but heatache like it vould pust open. Two, t'ree tays now I got dose heatache. I tells you plenty times alreatty. But I vork yoost da same ven I been so tissy I could fall down. Now you say I got it! Py cosh, I tell you plenty times—"

"Go look in the glass," some one advised him harshly. "Smallpox. You got it, you old fool."

LEN TAKES A HAND

UNTIL THAT MOMENT THE HAPPY FAMILY HAD NOT really believed the dreaded malady would actually appear among them. At the worst it had been only a threatened calamity which imposed certain restrictions upon them for a time and had given considerable physical discomfort. Down deep in their hearts they had clung to the conviction that it was just a scare. It would blow over and round-up would go on as always. The Jacksons would drive away to their own ranch, Bert would take Myrtle back to the Rogers ranch, Len and Bing Adams would ride home—and Bing would do that ploughing and planting which worried him so much. The coulee would seem kind of lonesome when they were gone, but the Little Doctor and Chip would come home with the kid, and that would help. All this quarantine business would resolve itself into one more adventure; nothing more.

All at once the adventure had taken a bad turn. The thing they didn't believe would really happen was now a fact that had to be faced. Shocked, slightly incredulous

74

still, the Happy Family squatted unhappily in the shade of the bunk-house and lighted cigarettes that went cold between their lips while they soberly discussed the situation. Weary had gone straight off to tell the Old Man and until he returned there was nothing to do but wait.

"This is sure going to knock spring round-up in the head," Pink broke a moody silence to remark. "We're bottled up for another two or three weeks, best we can do."

"Pore Bing. Them spuds of his'n won't git planted before frost, at this rate," Big Medicine contributed, with a wide grin that somehow failed to express amusement.

"We'll be c'relled here all summer, chances is," Happy Jack predicted with his usual pessimism. "I betcha we all come down with it. When I think of them biscuits we all et—"

"Gee whiz! Can't you talk about something else?" snarled Cal.

"Yeah. Quit yawping about them biscuits," Big Medicine admonished.

"I wisht now I'd 'a' saved out some of that sulphur we used on Nameless and the chicken mites," mourned Slim. "Now we ain't got a thing—"

"You're dead wrong," Andy cheerfully interrupted. "Doc brought a whole bunch of some kinda candles you burn with a special dew-dad that holds a white fumigating powder. You burn one in a room. Weary's went after one, I reckon."

"You fellows can josh me all you want to," Bing Adams spoke up suddenly. "Just the same, it does grind me to lay around over here, not doing a tap of work, and all that ploughin' waitin' over home. I ain't afraid of

75

catching it—it's spring work that bothers me."

"Oh, sure," drawled Andy, and sent a whimsically appraising glance around the solemn group. "That's all that any of us is worried about. There's just millions of things outside this coulee that we oughta be doing right now. Nameless is about the only one in the bunch that can't remember any important duties he's neglecting somewhere else—and what are you looking so white around the gills for, Nameless? You didn't eat a biscuit too, did yuh?"

"No, that isn't it at all." The pilgrim looked up from the tiny trench he was digging in the packed soil with a stick he had picked up. "I was just thinking of—well, there are ladies on this ranch—In a way, I'm responsible for the danger they're exposed to. If I had been killed instead of that poor horse, maybe everybody would be better off. They claim I was beating it away from my pal because I was yellow. Oh, I know it's in your minds, even if you don't say it. You all think this is my fault, even if I didn't come here of my own free will. In your hearts you blame me for running away from quarantine in the first place, and you blame Big Medicine here for bringing me to the ranch.

"As far as I'm concerned, I can't say anything because I don't remember why I was riding to the hills. There's just a vague feeling of something I had to do, no matter what happened. I don't believe I knew what ailed my partner when I left him. My honest belief is that when he saw he was too sick to travel any farther, he told me to go on alone and do whatever it was we had to do. I've thought and thought, till it seemed like I'd go crazy, but I can't bring back anything but just a vague feeling that there's something important—and I've failed to do it because I was brought down here and can't leave; and even if I could, I can't remember what it is I ought to do." He drew a long sigh, brushed his fingers across his eyes and dropped his hand with an inarticulate sound like a groan.

"I don't know as I ought to expect you fellows to believe a thing I say," he added dispiritedly, since no one spoke. "My memory may be gone, but I think I have brains enough left to see what I'm up against. You fellows have been kinda holding off, waiting to see if this smallpox business was a false alarm before you took any stand—"

"And what stand did you expect us to take?" Andy broke in to inquire. "Think we'd stand you up against the stable and shoot yuh, maybe?"

"Well, not exactly that, maybe. But—"

While he groped for words to express whatever vague forebodings troubled him at the moment, Weary came walking down the path with both hands full of small articles. So absorbed was he in the strict performance of his duty that he failed to notice the constrained silence. Or if he did, he probably attributed it to the misfortune that had just befallen the outfit.

"J. G. says for you boys to set up the bed tent down beyond that cottonwood by the creek," he announced, as he came up and stopped.

The Happy Family immediately rose and flicked fingers down thighs with the brushing gesture which outdoor men unconsciously use when they get up off the ground. That done, they resettled their hats on their heads and were ready for action.

"Don't set that tent close enough so the limbs 'll catch fire when we burn it afterwards," Weary gave further instruction. "Peg 'er down good and tight, because the Old Man thinks all this warm weather is breeding a storm. We better build a frame and take that set of springs in the blacksmith shop, so Patsy won't be laying right on the ground if it should rain. Trench around the tent, anyway; you jaspers need exercise.

"Soon as Patsy's moved outa the mess house, we can plug the cracks and light this gadget the doctor left. It's supposed to knock all germs cold in about four hours. Beats sulphur all to pieces, Doc said, but the powder in this paper is deadly poison, so I'll handle this end of the job myself. And we're supposed to run up a yellow flag. That's the smallpox signal, they tell me.

"Doc gave J. G. full instructions of what to do if a case broke out amongst us. The patient has got to be kept in bed, whether he feels sick or not. It's hell if yuh catch cold, he says. It ain't likely to be very bad, on account of everybody being vaccinated right away. And there's no use dodging old Patsy—everybody on the ranch was exposed that first day, with Nameless here. But the folks at the house think we better fumigate the mess house before we cook another meal there, just on general principles.

"So let's get busy. Andy, you and Mig can plant a pole and fly our flag of distress. Nameless, I'll let you and Bing help me plug up the mess house, and the rest of you fellows can get the tent ready. Put your flag up at one end of the tent, boys; we'll do this thing proper, accordin' to Hoyle, or we won't do it at all." He laughed, lowering an eyelid as if the whole affair might, after all, be only an amusing incident.

The tension relaxed as they scattered to their various tasks. When the girls came down a few minutes later to watch the tent go up, faces brightened and voices took on the vibrant note of merrymaking. Nameless and his trouble were pushed into the background of their minds.

Time enough for problems when they forced an issue. For the past week the girls had not ventured farther than the White House porch, for they too had suffered. Moreover, Rena's father was still in bed and likely to remain there for some time, because of some chronic ailment, and with J. G. weathering an attack of rheumatism, there had been plenty to do. Needless to say, they had been missed.

"The Countess is all right again now, and she chased us all out of the kitchen a little while ago, so I guess we'll have to strike you boys for a job of cooking," Len laughed.

"If you think you can make us mad that way, you're all off the track," grinned Cal.

"Yeah, we thought this was goin' to let us in for some of Happy's horrible mixtures," said Pink.

"Of course, you'll have to eat up at the house to-day; Countess is up to her eyebrows in cooking, and she was afraid to trust us to fry doughnuts, even."

"Just as if we never cooked in our lives!" Rena dutifully seconded the criticism.

"I'll back my doughnuts against anybody's," Len declared, more than half in earnest. "Myrt, here—why, where is she? I thought she was standing right over there watching Andy."

"She went off with Mig to rustle something yellow for a flag," Andy explained, looking up from the hole he was digging at the end of the tent.

"Better hang Mig awn that pole you're puttin' up," Big Medicine suggested. "He's about as yeller as anything awn the ranch." Not one stroke did he miss on the tent peg he was driving with the flat side of an axe.

"Nope," drawled Andy, mopping his face with a handkerchief white as a woman's. "I don't believe that

79

would work. Mig ain't limber enough to flop in the breeze."

Those within hearing laughed, just as he meant that they should. It seemed to him that Big Medicine was losing his sense of humor and making a grievance of everything the Native Son said or did. Not that the words themselves might not have been spoken a month ago—they would have been, probably, if the occasion had presented itself and Big Medicine had thought of them. But they would not have carried the venom that filled them now. It was hard to parry such savage thrusts and make them pass as a joke. Big Medicine wasn't joking and he seemed anxious to let it be known that he was not.

Len Adams looked at him with her steady gray eyes that just missed being some other color and moved over to Andy's side as he bent to his work.

"What's wrong?" she asked, just above a whisper. "Is he by any chance jealous of the Native Son?"

"Search me," Andy returned guardedly. "Might be just bilious; you can't tell."

Len sent a casual glance over her shoulder, saw that Big Medicine had finished with that tent peg and had gone to another down near the far corner where Rena stood talking, and leaned closer.

"You want to look out for Myrt Forsyth; all of you boys," she warned. "She flirted with him—I caught her at it when Mr. Jackson was so sick and Big Medicine was helping take care of him. And she makes fun of him behind his back, because he's so homely. She mimics the way he laughs that big 'haw-haw-haw-w-w', and then when he comes around she's sweet as pie. If you could give him a hint that she's just making a fool of him—"

"You want me to commit suicide?" Andy slanted a quizzical look up at her. "He'd blow my brains out, most likely."

"I don't see why. He'd know you were talking for his own good."

Andy straightened up to ease his back and to feel tenderly the sore muscles of his left arm. His eyes dwelt speculatively upon Len's earnest face.

"Sister," he said gravely, "you'd be surprised how many murders have been committed because some darn fool tried to talk to a man for his own good. I want to live. There's places to go and things to do I ain't gone and done yet."

"If you'd said 'things to tell', I'd be more impressed. And don't call me sister. Somebody ought to tell him she's just stringing him along. I hate to see a man made a fool of; a good-hearted fellow like Big Medicine. He ought to know he hasn't got a chance in the world with Myrt."

"How about Mig? Think she's got any time for him?"

"Well, I hope it won't hurt your feelings too much if I say Myrt is rather gone on our fine young Native Son. He's the best looking cowboy that ever rode this range, for one thing. And from the little I've seen of them together, he can sure put a lot of meaning into those velvet eyes of his."

"Myrt's no slouch herself when it comes to goo-goo eyes," Andy sighed, lifting the digger for another spasm of industry.

"So you've got a touch of it too!" Len eyed him curiously. "Well, you might better have smallpox, if you ask me."

"Now, don't you worry any about me." Andy tilted his head again to smile up at her. "Nor the rest of the boys, either," he added loyally, jabbing the digger deep and drawing it up carefully, so as not to spill any of the moist dirt it held. "Us poor cowboys may look simple and act simple, but you must remember there's always safety in numbers. We may cut each other's throats, so to speak, in the bosom of our own bunk-house, but nevertheless we hang together. *E pluribus unum*—the tail goes with the hide. You bet your life."

Len made a sound like a very ladylike snort. "That may all be very true—in fact, I know it is—but it doesn't work when a woman like Myrt comes into the coulee. If you don't tell him—" she indicated Big Medicine with a turn of her hand "—there'll be the Old Harry to pay. And if the rest of you fall for her—"

"We haven't so far. Not by a long shot."

"And do you know why?" Len leaned closer and spoke with a suppressed vehemence rather foreign to her. "Myrt hasn't bothered with the rest of you yet. I know it's awful to knock a person the way I am Myrt, but I don't care. Something's got to be done about Big Medicine. You've got to warn him, or something."

Andy once more caressed his sore arm.

"A fellow takes an awful chance, handing out warnings in love affairs," he said gravely. "For instance, if I was to warn you that Bert Rogers is about ready to murder me because we've been talking here by ourselves, and that if you don't give him a kind word before long—"

"Oh, you make me sick!" snapped Len and walked off toward the house.

Myrtle Forsyth and the Native Son were coming, heads close together and voices lowered, little wooing laughter breaking now and then through the soft monotone of their talk. Len met them and passed them without a look or word, and neither took the slightest notice of her nearness. Andy sent an oblique and searching glance toward Big Medicine. He was just in time to see him duck his high hat crown in under the flap of the tent where he might sulk unseen. Andy shook his head at that. It was not like Big Medicine to step out of the way of any one.

"We looked and looked and *searched* for a yellow cloth," Myrtle explained, as the two came up. "Then Miguel asked me why a *black* cloth wouldn't do, and I think it's the funniest thing I ever heard of, to use black when we really went after *yellow*. Do you suppose it will be all right? Because we really did search the whole place for a yellow—"

"Sure; anything," Andy said shortly, as if he were chiefly anxious to halt her italicized eloquence. "Tie it on that little end of the pole, there, and let's get the thing up and done with. The main thing is to serve notice, and the sooner the quicker."

So they flew the black flag of piracy, never dreaming how sardonically appropriate it was.

NAMELESS LOVES SOLITUDE

THE SPURIOUS CALM OF FORCED INACTION LAY UPON Flying U Coulee. These were the days when the Happy Family should have been riding the high green prairies, their tents pitched beside some clear flowing stream left behind for the next camping. Life should run free, with the clean winds blowing across new grass and bringing the scent of spring flowers, the sweet, high warbling of birds lately returned to the nesting places. Old Patsy should have been riding the lurching bed wagon, a huge deep pan of rising bread dough lashed to the seat beside him while he drove his four-horse team up the hills and down the hollows, hurrying to set up camp and have the next meal ready when the riders came galloping in.

Instead, the bed tent that should have been pitched in some remote wilderness sprawled in the open space beyond the cottonwood tree, the black flag casting sinister shadow upon its dingy gray roof. When hat crowns ducked into its doorway, voices invariably rose to profane argument against old Patsy's querulous complaints. Men came out of these scowling and muttering to themselves, and the tent walls quivered to the roll of German maledictions. As may be surmised, Patsy was not a particularly docile patient.

The Happy Family endured three days of this and told one another they had reached their limit. Then Bing Adams was discovered sprawled on his bed, suffering from what he called one of his sick headaches. Weary went after Len and Len immediately hurried to the bunk-house to investigate.

"It's all right, I guess," she reported, with studied cheerfulness. "Bing gets these spells every once in a while. All he ever wants is to be left alone. He'll sleep it off and be all right in the morning." And she went back to help with the supper.

Somewhat reassured, the boys lounged outside and played seven-up on a canvas spread under a tree where fluffs of cotton drifted down upon them from the tasseled branches. So far as appearances went, no one gave Bing Adams another thought. Just a common headache—too much eating and not enough work. Nothing to worry about.

But they must have betrayed themselves in spite of the unmerciful joking and laughter at the supper table, for suddenly Myrtle Forsyth broke into shrill, half-hysterical laughter.

"It's the *funniest* thing," she gasped. "The way you all talk and laugh and pretend you aren't the least bit worried—it's exactly like that book 'Delambre'!"

Three faces noticeably changed expression. The Native Son, lifting his cup to his lips, set it down abruptly without drinking. A slow flush crept from cheeks to brow. Nameless sent quick, sidelong looks to left and right of him, pulled in his lips at the corners and bent lower over his plate. Andy Green swallowed something down his "Sunday throat" and left the table hurriedly, knocking over a box as he retreated outside. The others waited for further enlightenment.

"What-all's that book about?" asked Big Medicine, his bellowing voice strangely belying the fatuous look in his frog eyes.

"Oh—it's an old classic," Myrtle hedged with some confusion. "It just tells about a lot of lords and ladies shut up in an old castle, just outside Paris or somewhere, waiting to see if they're going to have the *black plague.* All they did was make jokes and tell stories, just laughing at death in the *bravest* way, and pretending they didn't *care.*"

"And we kinda remind you of them, do we?" Andy, still red in the face from his mischance, straddled back into his place.

"Well, you *know* every one is wondering if Bing has the smallpox, and nobody dares to *mention* it—"

"You're dead right," said Weary, in a peculiar, steely tone. "Folks can talk themselves into all kinds of grief."

It was the first time Weary had voluntarily spoken to Myrtle direct, and the Happy Family pricked up their ears, waiting to see what would happen.

85

As a matter of fact, nothing did. Myrtle gave Weary a startled look, her eyes wider than she was in the habit of opening them, but her red lips came together in a thin line. With a toss of her bright auburn head she turned from the table and set the coffeepot on the stove without a word. The voice of Cal Emmett, asking some one to pass the pie, sounded loud in the silence.

Although no one seemed to know exactly what Weary meant, other than a rebuke of Myrtle's tactlessness, the constraint failed to relax. The Happy Family finished eating and filed out with scarcely a word to the girls. The pilgrim, however, lingered to ask if he could help with the dishes and Big Medicine turned back to offer his services also. Andy Green hesitated just outside the door, looking curiously at Myrtle, smiling up into Big Medicine's eyes. Then with an inarticulate exclamation, he hurried on to overtake Pink and Cal Emmett.

"Weary's got his back up, did yuh notice?" Cal remarked tentatively. "That Myrt ain't got a lick of sense, in some ways. Took old Weary to shut her up, though."

"Yeah. Only Weary didn't shut her up quite quick enough." He glanced at the two sidelong while he licked his cigarette into shape and fumbled for a match. "Either of you boys catch on to what Myrt was driving at—about that book?"

Pink shook his head. "I don't go much on classical reading," he confessed. "Them brainy old boys took too darn long to get to the point. And yuh need a dictionary right at your elbow to know what they're driving at."

"Not with that book you don't," Andy said drily.

"It's sure a bad time to talk about black plague," Cal observed tentatively. "That's what the book's about, Myrt said."

"Yeah, but that ain't what knocked me off my perch. Say, listen." Andy caught an arm of each and they walked slowly down the path, heads together while Andy talked in an undertone. Incredulous exclamations punctuated his monologue, with a great burst of laughter when he had finished.

"Gee whiz! If that's a classic—" Cal shook his head.

"You're just makin' it up as yuh go along," Pink made accusation.

"No, on the square. That's the book, all right."

"Where'd you ever read it?" Pink challenged.

"Over on the Cannon Ball. I was riding through that country and got stormbound in a line camp. They had the book."

Cal half turned to look over his shoulder at the mess house.

"And you'd think butter wouldn't melt in her mouth!" he made wondering comment, and shook his head again. "What made her tip her hand like that, d' you s'pose?"

"Thought we was all such ignorant cusses we wouldn't *sabe* anything but what she told us," Andy said promptly. "Myrt's scared, and the way we were all joshing and cutting up at the table made her think of that black plague party. She never expected some of the rest of us might read them old classics. Well, keep it under your hats, boys. I just had to tell somebody or bust."

He turned and retraced his steps to the bunkhouse, meaning to take another look at Bing. He found Weary there ahead of him, staring thoughtfully down at the flushed face on the pillow. He looked up as Andy came in, and his eyes were troubled.

"That's no sick headache," he muttered, drawing Andy back toward the door. "He was talking crazy as a loon when I came in a minute ago. Fever's a mile high.

87

We might as well go and fix another bed in the tent, don't you think?"

Andy tiptoed to the bunk and stood looking for a minute at Bing, then tiptoed back again.

"We might as well," he said reluctantly, and the two went out together.

They were carrying an old set of springs across the yard when the pilgrim trotted up to them, bare-headed and looking very well pleased with life.

"I don't know what the idea is in sleeping like sardines in a can," he began briskly. "You fellows can pack yourselves into that bunkhouse if you want to, but I'd like more fresh air than I'm getting at night. I want to take my blankets back up there in the grove, where I can hear the creek gurgle and the birds sing their morning how-de-do. Any objections, Boss?"

Weary, carrying the front end of the springs, shifted the awkward burden on his shoulders and gave the pilgrim a side-long glance from under his hatbrim.

"You can pack your bed as far as those boys on the ridges will let you," he said tersely. "By the creek or in the creek, it's all the same to me."

"Sure it's the beauties of nature you hanker for?" Andy inquired banteringly, steadying the springs while Weary got a new handhold.

"What do you mean by that?" The pilgrim whirled on him.

"Not a thing in the world," Andy disclaimed. "Only them same birds might take a notion to fly down this way to do their singin'. And the same water guggles right close handy by. You don't have to go way up past the White House to get fresh air, either. Of course, though, this might be too close to the sick—"

"No, that's got nothing to do with it," the pilgrim

88

denied. "Maybe I'm a poet or something—who knows? There's a place up there where the water falls down over rocks and the trees have left a clear space right beside it. I kinda fell for that spot the minute I saw it. Guess I'll go move my blankets up there before it gets dark." He started off, then called back to them with a forced laugh, "Yep, I must be a poet or something."

"Yeah—you're a liar or something," Andy muttered under his breath.

"Him and his warbling birds and gurgling brooks!" snorted Weary. "Why couldn't he say he's scared and be done with it? That's no disgrace—he's got plenty of company."

Andy kept careful pace with Weary, the rusted bed springs between them. At the tent they eased their load to the ground for a minute of rest.

"Say, did you ever read that book 'Delambre'?" he asked abruptly, his gray eyes turning for a thoughtful glance at Weary.

Weary's eyebrows came together. "No. Never heard of it before. Why?"

"Oh, nothing." Andy resettled his hat and stooped to lift the springs again. "I'll bet Nameless has read it," he said laconically, and followed Weary inside the tent.

WHISTLING RUFUS

WITHIN TWENTY-FOUR HOURS BING ADAMS HAD something to worry about more important than his ploughing. He was down in the hospital tent with old Patsy, and a cold drizzling rain was beating down upon the sodden canvas. Two of the boys in streaming yellow slickers brought hot food in a wash boiler with the lid pressed down to keep out the rain, and old Patsy grumbled and swore because the coffee was neither strong enough nor hot enough.

He wanted his camp stove that had gone with him on round-up every year since Jim Whitmore first ran his own wagons. He wanted his chuck box set inside the tent, and he wanted plenty of grub. He and Bing could make out all right without any woman's finger in their pie. Patsy did not put the matter in just those words, but that was his meaning, and he made it perfectly plain.

"Spuds mit onion and egg—und calls it salet," he spluttered. "I takes my spuds and cook 'im der vay I vants 'im, py cosh."

"You're getting well, that's all that ails you," Weary shrewdly diagnosed his complaining. "All right, have it your own way. If this rain lets up a little so we can do it, I'll have the boys set up your outfit here. Looks like this thing's going to hang on indefinite, and you might as well take charge of the hospital camp, Patsy. Save the rest of us a lot of legwork running back and forth, packing grub down here, and it'll give you something to do. The girls are making out fine cooking for the bunch. They'd hate to give it up unless they get sick—which I sure hope they don't."

Patsy had his own opinion about how three girls were handling the work in the mess house. He expressed his opinion freely to Bing after Weary was gone, but Bing was too sick to care what happened or how many dish towels were lost. He gave a surly grunt or two and turned his back, pulling the blankets up over his ears to shut out the sound of Patsy's voice. A clammy calm at last settled upon the tent. Patsy dozed or lay listening to the dulled patter of rain which seemed never to cease, and waited for the boys to bring his camp stove.

90

Not a soul came near until supper time. Then Cal brought a pot of coffee and a kettle of soup that lacked salt and hastily recounted the events of the day. The stove had smoked all afternoon and the girls had to beat it up to the White House and stay until the boys got things working again. They had been obliged to take down the pipe and clean it. The elbow was so full of "sut" that a puff of cigarette smoke couldn't have got through on a bet. Didn't Patsy ever clean his stovepipe? It sure looked like that sut had collected there for ten years. Well, then they had to take the darned stove to pieces, just about, and drag out the sut under the oven. It sure was a fright, having to do it in the rain. The darned stuff blew all over the place whenever any one opened the door, and you couldn't set a foot down anywhere without making black tracks. Cal was willing to bet that Patsy hadn't touched a scraper to that stove since it was bought.

Well, the place was like a barn all afternoon, and Len's bread didn't raise like it ought to, and the Countess didn't have but one loaf on hand. The girls were going to make biscuits for supper, but they thought maybe sick folks oughta have something hot right on time. So this was the best the girls could do right at present, and if they felt like they wanted something more after a while, the boys would bring something down when it was cooked.

With that cheering promise Cal retreated, his slicker crackling in the cold as he went. Bing and Patsy were still morosely discussing their wrongs when Weary and Pink appeared with a lantern and the inevitable wash boiler, wherein various dishes of food steamed appetizingly when the lid was lifted. They brought further news. Happy Jack was "on the lift," which in range parlance meant that he was down and couldn't get up. Or wouldn't. Weary believed he was sick, but Pink was inclined to the opinion that Happy was plain scared. They'd know all about it in the morning, he guessed.

The two did what they could for the comfort of the patients and departed, empty dishes rattling in the wash boiler. It was dark as a stack of black cats, they declared, and there was no sign of a let-up in the storm. But come hell or high water, Patsy should have his cook outfit next day. And by all the signs, Weary thrust his head back into the tent to say, they'd have company in the morning.

He was right. Next day it was plain to all who saw him that the thing which Happy Jack feared had come upon him. Wrapped like a mummy in canvas to keep him dry, he was carried down through the rain and put to bed, for the time being, with Bing.

All that forenoon yellow slickers went flapping here and there through a misty drizzle, making endless trips to meet old Patsy's querulous demands. The Happy Family grumbled a good deal, but when the task was finished they agreed that it was worth the trouble and that it solved a growing problem very satisfactorily. They had left the tent warm and crudely comfortable, with old Patsy pottering about the stove, stirring certain savory mysteries that carried the odor of range cooking. Slim, who lingered to stack a generous supply of wood in the corner behind the stove, sniffed hungrily and hinted at staying for dinner, but Patsy drove him out.

"Mamma!" Weary exclaimed earnestly, as he and Pink left the tent after a neighborly visit that afternoon. "It's sure going to be a big relief, the way things are fixed now. That'll keep old Patsy outa the mess house till this quarantine lets up. Gives the girls a free hand. I've been wondering how I could work it so they could go on cooking for the bunch. This way, it's fine."

"Fine for them that are well," Pink amended. "But it's sure tough on the feller that's sick. If I get smallpox, I hope I spend the whole entire time unconscious. If I've got to be waited on and pawed over by old Patsy, I don't want to know it."

"All right, Cadwalloper. I'll bear that in mind," Weary grinned. "A gentle tap on the head with an axe every morning oughta do. Anything to save your feelings."

Just then they met Andy coming up from the stable. He too was full of optimism in spite of the weather. He fell into step beside them and took up the conversation from his own angle.

"What d' yuh know about it? Bert wiped the dishes for Len. Looks like the ice is kinda thawing there, don't yuh think?"

"I'd want to see it myself," Pink discounted the statement.

"All right, you can ask Mig. Him and Nameless played euchre with Myrt and Rena while Len and Bert washed the dishes. The lion and the lamb—"

"Tell another one," Weary interrupted.

"It's a fact. I never said how long the game lasted, you notice. Myrt got 'em started in the first place. Mig and Bert was foolin' around in there and Nameless showed up, so Myrt boned them for a game and neither one would back down for the other. They must've played for a full ten minutes before it was necessary to create a diversion."

"How was that?"

"Hunh? Oh, I forget just how it happened. I sure do hope it clears up so Nameless can go back to his birds and flowers. Or if he'd come down with smallpox, even—"

"What you got against Nameless?" Weary demanded. "Barring he's a kind of smart aleck, I can't see anything wrong with him."

"By gracious, I'm suspicious of a guy there's nothing wrong with." Andy's rain-washed countenance looked stubborn. "He's such an agreeable cuss I'm getting darn sick of him. There's something about him—if I could remember what it was—"

"Well, I wouldn't bother much about things I couldn't recall," said Weary. "Take him as he comes, why can't you? He's all right, I guess."

From the mess house as they approached came the reedy notes of a harmonica mingled with the throbbing of a guitar playing chords in D with Slims well-known variations. As they turned into the muddy path from the bunk-house there came, high and clear above these familiar sounds, the tones of a flute. The three looked at one another inquiringly, then Weary pushed open the door.

Inside the long, low room the Flying U boys were perched on the table or sprawled at ease on the nearest long bench. Cal and Slim were playing "The Mocking Bird," and lounging against the wall near them stood Nameless with his arms folded. The music they had called a flute came from the pursed lips of the pilgrim, whistling a tenor obligato with a bird song interlude.

The boys stood staring at him in amazement until Len raised her hand and beckoned, signalling for silence in eloquent pantomime. So they tiptoed across the open space to the stove, where they stood steaming until the music was ended and they might divest themselves of slickers and overshoes.

"Isn't that perfectly *wonderful?*" Myrtle's clear treble inquired above the stamping and clapping. "And he's

94

been here all this while, and never once *hinted* he was such a perfectly divine whistler!"

"I didn't know it myself—if you call that divine," Nameless replied, with the proper degree of modesty in his tone. "I just happened to get started, I reckon. Lemme have that guitar a minute, Slim. I feel another one coming on and I've got a hunch I can play for it myself."

"He knows darn well he can," Andy whispered suddenly to Pink. "Say, I know what it was I couldn't remember—"

But Pink shook his head rebukingly and nudged Andy into silence. The pilgrim was whistling the "Miserere" with a haunting lament in the tones, a trembling despair that made even the Native Son bite his lip. They knew the piece well enough. The Little Doctor had a complete set of "Il Trovatore" records up at the White House, with the story of the opera. But not even the record produced quite that effect of imminent tragedy.

He should have stopped then, while they marvelled at the sheer genius of his performance. But he did not. He was a little excited by his triumph perhaps; a shade too greedy for applause. He whistled several selections without pause, watching the faces of the girls for the homage in their shining eyes. He imitated almost perfectly the robin's song, the wild canary, the sweet warble of the meadow lark. "Now you see why I wanted to sleep up there in the grove," he interrupted himself to remark, with a challenging glance at the Native Son. Immediately afterwards he whistled "The Swallow Song" without missing one intricate trill or blurring a liquid grace note.

He was like an indefatigable canary which, however lovely his song, must finally be subdued with a cloth

95

over his cage. The spell cast by the poignant perfection of the "Miserere" was gone. Boots began to move restlessly upon the bare floor. Slim rolled and lighted a cigarette and flipped the match stub at Bert Rogers, and because it landed on Bert's nose Rena Jackson giggled audibly. Glances wandered, bored listeners seeking mental diversion. And suddenly the pilgrim broke off in the middle of a phrase and thrust the guitar into Slims arms.

"Play us a waltz, boys," he cried gayly, flashing a signal into Myrtle Forsyth's watchful eyes.

"You bet! Play '*Sobre las Olas*'." Like a young seal slipping from an ice floe, the Native Son slid down from the table and swung Myrtle into the rhythm of the dance. With a concerted movement that seemed inspired, Andy Green and Pink captured Len and Rena and went waltzing down upon the pilgrim, their faces blandly innocent.

Nothing was left for the pilgrim except to back into a corner out of the way. Even so, he did not back quickly enough. As Myrtle swished past in the arms of the Native Son, Miguel's boot-heel come down with considerable force on the pilgrim's toes. Miguel instantly begged to be excused for the accident and whirled his partner away. The pilgrim drew a sharp hissing breath between his clenched teeth and bided his time.

The waltz ended with a flourish, but the musicians left little interval. Cal, in fact, merely gave himself time to moisten his lips before he began playing a schottische. Again the pilgrim started forward, but his corner was blocked—inadvertently we hope—by Weary, who drew back to give Bert Rogers elbow room with Rena Jackson. By the time Weary realized that

Nameless wanted to pass, the three girls were already dancing. Weary apologized, but that did not alter the situation in the least. Again the pilgrim waited, eyes gleaming.

Other dances followed in rapid succession, but somehow Weary, Bert Rogers, Andy and Pink were always before him, eager to dance, and fortunate in having Len or Rena at least every other time. And without any apparent design or collusion, Myrtle Forsyth seemed always accepting the Native Son for a partner just before the pilgrim reached her side. The system of cutting in was not established at that time, unless due notice was served by the floor manager who might announce a "tag" waltz or two-step. Cal didn't make that announcement. It was a case of get a partner or keep out of the way. Though he may not have realized it until the affair was over, the pilgrim never had a chance.

"Oh, stop it, for pity's sake!" Len gasped at last, reeling dizzily against Bert Rogers and blushing furiously at the contact. "Don't dance us to death—there's supper to get."

"Play 'Whistling Rufus'," the Native Son called clearly above the noise. "Myrt and I want to cakewalk to that tune before we stop!"

Slim and Cal looked at each other dubiously, but the Native Son was waiting with his partner in the middle of the floor and Cal licked his sore lips and began the rollicking tune. The onlookers pressed backward to give space, and the two came stepping and swaying down the room, elbows flapping, heads tilted—

The door slammed upon the pilgrim's departure, and a moment later Big Medicine followed him out, turning in the doorway to glare furiously at the Native Son, who

97

met his look with an extravagant salute that might have been an integral part of the dance but probably wasn't. Not for nothing had Bud Welch of Coconino County Arizona been rechristened Big Medicine. The glaze in his pale, protruding eyes promised much as he slammed the door behind him.

Then Len Adams, who was normally a sensible girl, did a very foolish thing. She pounced unexpectedly upon Cal and dragged the harmonica away from his mouth.

"Beat it, you boys! You've made those two sore with your joshing and you ought to be ashamed. Clear out now, the whole entire bunch of you. Scat—vamoose— beat it, I tell you! Rena, hand me that broom!"

Whereupon the chortling Happy Family grabbed hats and slickers and surged out into the rain, uproariously singing the chorus of that grotesquely appropriate song which the Native Son had recklessly flung at the pilgrim:

> "Didn't make no blun-der
> > You couldn't confuse him—
> A perfect won-der,
> > You had to choose him!
> A great musician
> Of high position
> > Was Whistling Rufus, the one-man band!"

BIG MEDICINE DECLARES WAR

" 'Way down south in the land of cotton
  And the home of the syc-amore tree-ee
Lived a darky called Rufus Blossom,
  Black as a nigger could be-ee.
Had a head like a big sledge hammer
  And a mouth like a horrible scar-rr,
But nothin' could touch him in Ala-bama
  When he played on his old guit-ar-r!
"Didn't make no blun-der,
  You couldn't confuse him—"

STILL SINGING AT THE TOP OF THEIR VOICES, THE BOYS burst tunefully into the bunk-house. Big Medicine, walking the floor like a man-eating lion pacing his cage before feeding time, halted his stride and glared.

"—A per-fect won-der,
  You had to choose him—"

sang the Native Son, mirth in his velvet eyes as he approached.

"Say, you damn' black-an'-tan Romeo—" Big Medicine bellowed truculently, and got no farther, because the Native Son's fist smashed the words back into his wide mouth.

"That for you, Frog-eyes," hissed Miguel, his eyes no longer mirthful. "No man with a drop of Castilian blood in his veins ever swallowed that insult."

99

"You'll swallow worse'n that," bawled Big Medicine, lunging forward. "Anybody that'll do the dirty trick you done to Nameless—" He landed a glancing blow on Miguel's shoulder and got one in return that made him grunt.

"Say, why don't you let Nameless fight his own battles, Bud?" Weary remonstrated. "He ain't crippled."

"Nameless kin finish—what I leave," Big Medicine panted, circling like a dancing bear. "I got plenty reasons—" What they were he did not state, chiefly because Miguel's fist that instant landed neatly on his nose.

With an inarticulate bellow he drove at the Native Son. They clinched and struggled and jabbed, tore apart suddenly and fought furiously with their fists. The Happy Family kept out of their way and watched with silent disapproval. There was no just cause for all this enmity. Until the disturbing foreign element entered Flying U Coulee, these two had always been the best of friends. Nameless and Myrtle Forsyth—one to breed distrust and the other jealousy, and neither apparently giving a thought to the trouble each had caused.

"Hey, cut it out, you fellows!" Weary suddenly shouted above the noise of combat. "Pile in there, boys—this has gone far enough!"

Pink, Andy Green and Cal rushed in upon Big Medicine. Weary, Bert Rogers and Slim attempted to hold Miguel. It was a mistake. They found themselves involved in a struggle with two contending demons who made no distinction between friend and foe. Blows aimed at a foe too often fell upon a friend whose temper was not proof against pain. Abruptly the peacemakers were fighting in one terrible melee, with Miguel and Big Medicine still concentrating upon their own affair, their thirst for blood unassuaged.

Into the uproar walked the pilgrim. Two or three of the boys remembered afterwards that he stood for a moment with his back to the wall, sizing up the battle with cool, darting glances this way and that. Beyond that point opinions differed as to his mode of procedure, though it was agreed that Nameless kinda waded through the bunch and that the result was surprising.

"There's one thing I wisht I knew," Slim solemnly observed a little later, when the Happy Family had withdrawn to the stable to talk things over. "Where'd Nameless git all them arms from? He was hittin' four ways to oncet, by golly. I seen him."

"I tried to tell you boys," Andy complained, "but you wouldn't listen to me. I know all about that guy now. I can tell you—"

"Don't tell me anything," Pink interrupted him crossly, and gingerly caressed a swelling jaw. "I know plenty about that jasper right now."

"Well, but listen a minute! Nameless—"

"Aw, shut up about Nameless," snarled Bert Rogers. "We can take a fall outa that guy any time. Where's Mig? He's the boy I'm worrying about right now. If ever I saw murder in a man's eyes—"

"Oh, that's all right," Weary assured him, glancing up from inspecting a skinned knuckle. "Brown eyes like Mig's always look deadly when a fellow's mad. Mig will get over it."

"Don't fool yourself," Bert warned. "Not when there's a girl like Myrt eggin' 'em on all the while. It wasn't the way we got to runnin' on Nameless that made Big Medicine see red. It was Mig dancing with Myrt."

"Say," Cal spoke up, "what's the penalty for breakin' outa quarantine?"

"You thinkin' of making a sneak?" Slim asked uneasily. "You better not let them guards upon the hill ketch yuh at it, by golly. They'd shoot yuh down like a dog."

"Well, I was just thinkin' we might slip some uh these trouble makers outa the coulee some dark night. Haze Myrt and Nameless outa here and we'd get along fine."

"Not Nameless," Andy Green objected quickly. "We want to hang onto him, boys. He—"

"Hanging on ain't the problem," sighed Weary. "It's the lettin' go. Mamma, but that boy's a sure-enough wildcat. I kinda admire the way he walked into the bunch of us. No ifs nor ands nor asking who's to blame—he hears Big Medicine bellering and in he comes."

"And out we go," sighed Pink. "So help me Josephine, some day I'm going to take that pilgrim—"

"Wait till I tell yuh—" Andy Green made one more attempt to enlighten them.

"Aw, forget it," Cal implored. "You can't tell us anything we don't know, and if you could, we wouldn't believe it."

"All right, have it your own way," snapped Andy. "If you'd rather collect information by hand, go to it." He turned and stalked out, just as the Native Son emerged from the corral, leading a saddled horse.

"That you, Mig? Where you headed for?" Andy spoke guardedly, walking up to him.

"No law against riding down in the pasture, is there?" Miguel's voice was cold and unfriendly. He did not look at Andy when he spoke.

"Wait a second. I'll go along if you don't mind." Andy held his voice to a casual tone.

"Why?"

Andy did not answer the challenge directly. "I'll go crazy if I don't get a horse under me pretty quick," he complained. "The boys are back in the empty box stall, chewing the rag like a bunch of old women at a quilting bee. There's been too darned much chin-whacking on this ranch lately to suit me. 'Course," he digressed in his disarming fashion, "I don't have to ride with you if you're set on going by your lonesome; I can ride up the creek and you can ride down, or whichever way you want. But on the square, I hate to give up the idea of joggin' around a little—"

"Oh, cut out the argument and come along." Miguel's voice had thawed appreciably. "I'm not good company, *amigo*. I am trying not to think too much about killing."

"Then there's two of us," growled Andy. "I had to get out or start shooting."

Miguel gave him a sharp, suspicious look, but Andy stood the test, standing with clenched hands and his mouth pressed into a thin, straight line. His kindly gray eyes were hidden by his hat-brim. Miguel's glance turned toward the stable.

"Lead your horse around the corner of the corral outa sight till I throw my hull on a cayuse," Andy directed in the same low tone of repressed fury.

Miguel started, glanced at him again and did as he was directed. Within two or three minutes Andy appeared beside him, leading a gentle little bay horse by the reins. Without a word the two mounted, then held their horses quiet in the shadows while five indistinct forms emerged from the stable and went off up the path, their voices jumbled in argumentative discussion.

103

With the evening a moist wind blew out of the west, pushing the heavy clouds before it. In the widening patches of clear purple sky pale stars shone timidly. The creek had risen with the rain that for two days had sluiced down from the surrounding hills. Its voice was lifted from the sleepy murmur they knew best to a rushing monotone. With a tacit understanding of the way they would go, the two swung aside from the ford and followed the line of tangled bushes down the wet trail that led to the lower pasture.

In certain low places the creek had lipped out over its banks into the grove. Willows and chokecherry thickets stood knee-deep in muddy water. Occasionally the horses dropped heads to snuff the flooded trail, sometimes turning of their own accord to swing wide of boggy ground. On either hand the coulee walls rose steeply, and where the road to Dry Lake climbed the north rim two tents showed as white blotches in the dusk. Between them a camp fire sent up orange-tinted flames.

"Wonder where they get their wood," Andy speculated, like a man whose thoughts have pulled away from grimmer things.

His face was turned that way to watch the flickering yellow firelight, but he nevertheless saw Miguel leave off staring fixedly straight ahead of him and send an uninterested glance up to the camp of the guard.

"Old ties, chances are," Andy answered his own implied question. "Sure don't burn like wet brush."

The Native Son returned to his unseeing stare between his horse's ears and for another quarter mile no word was spoken. The two rode slowly, their horses walking shoulder to shoulder like a harnessed team. Now and then Andy's stirrup touched the stirrup of Miguel; evenly, since both hung on a level length adjusted to the straight legs of men owning full six feet of vital bone and flesh between hat and heels. *Clink*—a dull, small sound; an inarticulate little voice hinting that here rides a friend. *Clink—clink—a* companionable little sound in the dark. The faint jar of contact somehow carried sympathy, understanding, a comradeship felt but never to be put into words.

Small groups of vague, grazing animals scattered before their approach. These were for the most part the half-broken saddle horses gathered from the range for the round-up that would not be made this spring. Already "reps" had been appointed by the Stock Association to ride for the Flying U. In a lighter mood this reminder would have stimulated profane discussion of the misfortune that had befallen the Happy Family, but to-night they rode without comment; until one wild group ducked and snorted, taken unawares behind a clump of brush.

"I believe that's the buckskin that piled Happy, that first Sunday," Andy remarked, twisting in the saddle for a better look as the horse galloped away. From the tail of his eye he saw that Miguel turned to glance after the horse.

He faced forward again, fingering his coat pocket and drawing out tobacco sack and cigarette papers. In somber silence he sifted tobacco into the tiny paper trough held steady in his fingers. With the manner of one who automatically performs an act of courtesy, he offered the tobacco sack and the papers to Miguel. But the trembling of his hand would have betrayed him to a man less absorbed in his own thoughts, and the sharp breath he drew was eloquent of relief when, after an appreciable moment of waiting, the Native Son pulled his thoughts from their bitter meditations and took the makings with a muttered "Thanks."

105

Smoking in silence, they rode as far as they might go without challenge from the guards who watched the coulee at its lower end. When they could hear voices and see the figures of men moving in the zone of firelight they turned aside, riding across sodden pasture land to the coulee's southern wall. And with a second cigarette between his handsome lips, Miguel turned and gave Andy a long, attentive look.

"To-night I nearly killed a man. Two men." His voice was calm, the tone almost casual.

"Uh-huh."

"I had left my gun in the saddle shed where I hung it the other day."

"Sure. I know. Saw it there to-day."

"When I met you at the gate I was almost decided I would go up and shoot those two and ride—to the Wild Bunch."

"Well, you didn't," Andy stated mildly.

"No, I didn't. Now I see I was *loco*. You've helped me to my senses. Such things are not forgotten, *amigo*."

"It was mainly our fault, Mig. We joshed too hard. I guess we all of us had a touch of *loco* weed lately. Kinda throwed off our base with all these happenstances." He laughed under his breath, wanting to lighten his words. "I reckon the air is cleared considerable now. We all of us had some fight bottled in our systems. We sure oughta act like humans from now on."

"*Si, señor*," Miguel said mockingly to hide his deeper emotions. "I shall not ride to the Wild Bunch. I stay here and have smallpox perhaps and spoil my beauty."

106

ANDY TELLS A SECRET

THEY RODE SLOWLY ALONG, SMOKING AND TALKING in the old way. The cold constraint had left Miguel's voice, his rigid pose in the saddle relaxed. In the starlight Andy's watchful eyes saw once more the familiar swing of the Native Son's body riding at negligent ease. They passed the ranch buildings a long rifle-shot away, but although their gaze clung to the dim clustered lights, neither suggested riding straight across to the corral and to their supper. Andy was busy talking, and Miguel was lounging in the saddle, one foot hanging free of the stirrup, his rein hand resting on the horn while he smoked and listened.

"You aren't stringing me, Andy?"

"Not on your life. I'd have placed him long ago, only I was about half-shot all the while I was in Minot. A girl had double-crossed me and I rode straight to town and got drunk—you know." Andy flapped a hand and Miguel nodded. "It was that whistling that cinched it. Drunk or sober, you couldn't forget a jasper that whistles the way he does."

"Never heard better," Miguel paid honest tribute. "It was his sublime conceit that—"

"Yeah, I know. That's him, all over. Plays to the gallery a lot—but he delivers the goods; you got to admit that." He smoked thoughtfully for a moment.

"So that's his brand," he continued. "Just a plain ordinary brakie, far as any one knew, till the thing was over. All the shopmen and railroaders backed him—and boy, how they cleaned the town! Got as high as four-to-one on Slim, as they called him. It never come out till

107

afterwards that Slim the brakie was Larry Jones, champ with a pedigree as long as your arm."

"Boxing, eh?" The Native Son touched a painful spot on his cheek bone.

"I'll say a boxer! *And* wrestler—*and* foot racer—the way he come streaking past the grandstand was as pretty a sight as a man ever looked at. They all et his dust that day. But, boy, was they sore! When it come out who he was, they'd 'a' mobbed him sure as fate. But Larry jumped a blind baggage and got outa the country." Andy flicked his cigarette with a finger nail and chuckled to himself. "I lost forty-five dollars on that jasper," he recalled whimsically. "That's a lot of money for a poor cowpuncher, Mig. Even if I was drunk, it hurt."

"Larry Jones, the whirlwind athlete!" The Native Son's tone was a study in mixed emotions. " 'Loping Larry!' "

"That's him—I'd back my last simoleon on it. And if he's as good as he was three years ago in Minot—"

"He got into some jangle with the athletic clubs on the Coast, just before I left," Miguel remembered. "Gave up athletics, I heard." He laughed suddenly. "His lost memory!" he jeered. "I knew there was something he was keeping under cover. He's a foxy one, amigo. I felt all along he was playing us for suckers."

"Maybe not that so much," Andy dissented. "Look what he was up against. Him and his pardner likely intended to get work in Dry Lake and lay low for Labor Day. He ain't a professional any more—you say yourself he gave that up. But he's just as good as ever, and willin' to pick up any little money he can make that way. It's like buying an old race horse for the farm, and then entering him at the county fair and making a clean-up. Nobody peddles records beforehand. If I had the

108

stuff Nameless has got, I'd figure on making money on my talents too."

"It was a raw deal he got on the Coast," Miguel admitted.

"Well, there you are. Jones is a common name. He coulda used it here and we wouldn't of connected him with Larry Jones. Well, somewhere along the line, him and his pardner picked up a mess of smallpox germs. That upset their apple cart right as soon as they landed. The pardner is laid out, and likely he framed it with Nameless to beat it outa town and lay low till things kinda got straightened out. Big Medicine picks him up and packs him in to the ranch, and while he's playin' for time and stallin' us off with his loss uh memory, here they come and slap the hull outfit into quarantine. Now his pardner's dead and he's got to look out for himself. What would you do, Mig, in his place?"

"Go right along with the plan," Miguel said promptly, "if I had the stomach for it in the first place. He can do it, unless we—"

"Which we won't," Andy leaned and caught Miguel's arm in an arresting grip. "Nameless he is and Nameless he shall remain, far as I'm concerned." He laughed gleefully. "You and me, Mig, can break even with that Dry Lake bunch that slipped the race horse over on us last year. All we got to do is look wise and say nothing. Let Loping Larry handle this in his own way; he sure oughta know his own game by this time. We got a grandstand seat, boy."

The Native Son made himself another smoke, lighted up and rode along in complete silence for a time.

"And how about the other boys?" he asked at last.

"Well, by gracious, I tried my darnedest to put 'em wise," Andy said resentfully "They wouldn't let me.

109

They said they wouldn't believe a word I said, anyhow."

"So the secret lies between us two?"

"That's what. There ain't another soul that knows, except Nameless, and he'll be the last to spill it. The rest can turn gray-headed waiting for me to tell 'em."

"Or for me, *amigo*," Miguel said softly, and blew a long silvery wisp of smoke neatly from his nostrils.

The sky was swept clear of clouds, save here and there a wispy streamer scudding across the Milky Way. The wind freshened.

"She'll be fine weather to-morrow," Andy predicted cheerfully. "We oughta be able to wrassle bronks if this wind keeps up. It'll dry the ground quicker than sun."

"What if Big Medicine—"

"Aw, forget it, Mig. Poor old Bud means all right. We been running him pretty hard, ever since he lugged the pilgrim in. I can see his side, all right."

"His side is damn rough, you must admit."

"Well, let him beller. Knowing what we know, this'll be good as a circus. It'll sure tickle me to watch Nameless perform with that lost memory. But remember, Mig, we keep this under our hats. Is it a go?"

"It's a go. I can hold my tongue."

"Yeah," said Andy slyly, "but how about your temper?"

"That too. I turn both cheeks and my back, *amigo*. You will see."

They had reached the upper end of the coulee. Now they turned back, shaking their horses into a gallop over the springy sod. "Yep, she'll be a fine day," cried Andy. "There'll be things doing in this old corral, boy."

There were fewer lights now. The mess house was dark, but they went in, lighting their way with matches until they found the lamp. The room was warm, the air heavy with the odor of cooking. A whitening bed of coals remained in the stove and the coffeepot stood near the pipe. Two places were set at the end of the long table nearest the stove, mute evidence that they were expected to return and eat their supper.

"Pot roast and spuds, Mig," Andy announced, lifting the lid of a kettle still comfortably warm. "Shall I heat up the coffee? What d' yuh think?"

"Set it in on the coals, *amigo*. Here's warm bread. I knew it was that I smelled." With his big hat pushed to the back of his head, the Native Son was haggling thick slices from a hot loaf. "Get the syrup can," he ordered, without lifting his eyes from his work. "How's the coffee, Andy?"

"Comin' up. How many spuds? No use making a lot of dishes to wash."

"Two, and plenty of gravy."

"You're on."

With the syrup can between them and the lamp wick turned too high; with their hats on the backs of their heads and their elbows on the table—throwing off all restraint like two runaway boys—they were mopping their plates with the last slices from the loaf when Weary opened the door and walked in. Behind him came Pink and Bert Rogers, anxious-eyed and slightly battered. They halted just within the door and their faces showed tremendous relief.

"Where the dickens have you been?" Bert demanded bluntly. "We'd about decided to take the mess wagon and round you up."

"Yeah," said Pink. "Where'd you go?"

"Hither and thither," drawled Andy, hurrying to take a bite of bread before the syrup dripped over the edge.

111

"There and thereabouts," the Native Son further elucidated. "I've got to have more bread to finish the syrup. How about you, *amigo*?"

"Nope. I need more syrup to come out even on the bread. And by gracious, I'm full to my eyebrows right now."

"Mamma!" Weary exclaimed in a baffled tone. "The darn chumps'll eat till they bust. Come on, boys, leave 'em at it,—I'm going to bed."

With a last wondering stare, the three departed. Andy and Miguel waited until they were gone, then looked at each other and grinned.

TROUBLE IN PLENTY

THEIR GOOD HUMOR HELD THROUGH THE NIGHT. AT breakfast their eyes met in glances of secret amusement across the table, and when the pilgrim came in late, his face glowing from his run and from his ablutions in cold water, Miguel was the first to slide the meat platter toward him.

"Have a nice run after the rain, Rufus?" he inquired, his tone warm and friendly.

"Rufus?" The pilgrim's eyes scrutinized him while he held the platter in one hand, his fork poised in the other.

"Whistling Rufus," the Native Son explained gently. "You can't get along without a name, *amigo*. Why not Rufus? Rufus—Jones." His velvet eyes dwelt innocently upon the other's blank face.

"There's something you need worse than a name," Andy put in hastily, seeing Big Medicine's wide mouth opening for speech that would probably make trouble. "You sure oughta learn to ride a horse."

"My own feet carry me pretty well," said the pilgrim, a guarded glance flashing to Andy.

"Yeah, I know. But in this country a man's got to be a rider. If you stay with the outfit you'll have to go on round-up—or you'll most likely want to—"

"Say, by cripes! What—"

"—and you oughta get Big Medicine to learn you how to ride and throw a rope. Bud's got his failings," Andy explained extenuatingly, "but there ain't a better rider in the outfit. I'll leave it to the bunch."

The Happy Family, stealing uneasy glances at one another, refused to be drawn into the discussion. Big Medicine gasped, his pale, protruding stare going from Andy to Miguel.

"Well, it might not be a bad idea at that," the pilgrim cautiously admitted. "I'll have to find a job somewhere—"

"Bud, what you ought to do is catch up a gentle horse and start Rufus right in," Miguel offered further suggestion. "He's bright and active and he ought to learn easy. Pass the syrup, will you, Bert?"

Big Medicine made an inarticulate sound and swallowed his coffee too hot. His broad face crimsoned to his bristling tow hair. He spluttered, damned the coffee in a whisper so that Len and Rena would not hear, and shot a suspicious glance around the table, hoping to catch an eye that would signal some key to the mystery; but the eyes of the Happy Family were attending to their breakfast.

"I don't need no advice—not even if it come from a—from a friend."

Slim gave a snort of strangled mirth at the hasty and wholly inadequate termination of Big Medicine's declaration. Len Adams had appeared suddenly at his elbow with fresh pancakes.

"Excuse it, then. It seemed to me that on this bright morning would be the time when Rufus should learn to ride. I meant no offence, I assure you." Never had the Native Son's smile been more brilliantly disarming, his eyes more innocent.

Big Medicine gave him a bewildered stare. There was a shuffling of feet on the floor, a general shifting of positions on the long benches. Cal Emmett's china-blue eyes grew perfectly round and void of all expression. Pink dimpled, then scowled as some one kicked him on the shin.

"It's a darned good idea," the pilgrim suddenly declared. "If you ask me, it's a da—*amned* good idea—" whispering the last syllable of the swear word while he cast a wary glance over his shoulder. "Rufus goes with me too. Brown, Smith, Jones—Rufus Jones could be a lot worse. Thanks, Mig, for the name. And I'll just take you up on the riding lesson."

"Not me, *amigo*," the Native Son declined in his silkiest tone. "Some one you trust."

"Well, by golly!" gasped Slim, and subsided under the malevolent stare which Cal Emmett gave him across the table.

"Sure going to be a fine day to-day if it don't rain to-morrow," Len Adams made flippant comment as she approached the table once more—this time with the coffeepot. "What's wrong with you fellows? You've been as solemn as a flock of moulting owls ever since you went and bunged each other up in that boxing contest yesterday." She stood at the end of the table, studying their faces as if she were a country schoolteacher and they were small boys suspected of hiding horned toads in their desks. "One-two-three black eyes, enough skin missing from the crowd to

114

cover a saddle, and thr—four cut lips—you're certainly the biggest herd of lump-jaws I ever saw in my life. If it's catching—"

"It sure is," murmured Weary, his head bent low over his plate.

"It sure looks it. Nameless is the only one in the bunch that had sense enough to keep out of the contest."

"Oh, mamma!" shuddered Weary, whispering to his hotcakes the astonishment he dared not express aloud.

"You'd better pattern your behaviour after him, from now on, and don't play so rough. Andy Green," she charged abruptly, thrusting the coffeepot toward him in an accusing gesture, "have you been up to anything?"

"Me? No, ma'am." Andy rolled meek eyes up at her.

"Just the same, you look guilty, you're so heavenly innocent."

"No, mom, you wrong me."

"Oh. You're *not* heavenly innocent! Was it you that left my bread uncovered to dry out? If the crust is hard as alder chips, don't blame me. I'm not saying a word about one whole loaf missing and the syrup can being almost empty, but when my bread is left uncovered—"

"Teacher!"

To the astonishment of his fellows, the Native Son confessed to that crime and to others which he invented upon the spot with fantastic details rivaling even that prince of liars, Andy Green. His sins were so many and his penitence so abject that Len threatened to brain him with the coffeepot—to put him out of his misery, she explained.

The diversion served its purpose. Under cover of their foolery the Happy Family hurriedly finished their breakfast and filed out into the clean-washed air of early morning. In May the rangeland is a green world filled

115

with the scent of wild flowers and the songs of birds. Already the sun shone into Flying U Coulee with a warmth that set the moist ground steaming. Upon the tip of the pole that held the black flag fluttering in the breeze a meadow lark perched and sang his sweet, brief ripple of song, tilted his head to one side and repeated the melody again and again without varying a note.

Len Adams in the doorway listened wistfully, the laughter gone from her lips and her eyes shadowed with worry. The soft air lifted brown tendrils of hair from her forehead, touched caressingly the line where her white forehead met the tan. She never felt that breeze. Her eyes following the group of long-limbed cowboys walking down the slope to the corrals with occasional brief halts while they applied flaming matches to their new-made cigarettes. Rena Jackson, coming to stand beside her, looked and laughed.

"Boxing contest!" She laughed again. "If there wasn't a free-for-all fight in the bunk-house after they left here yesterday, I miss my guess. I wonder what it was all about."

"Oh, you do!" Len twitched herself free of Rena's embracing arm. "I suppose when there's a killing over Myrt Forsyth, you'll wonder what that's about too." She pointed a finger after the retreating group. "Look how they're pairing off. You never used to see that kind of thing going on amongst the Flying U boys, did you? Big Medicine and Nameless don't have anything much to do with the rest, you notice; and it's Big Medicine that worries me, Rena. With all the fooling and cutting up this morning, he never laughed once. I tried my darnedest to make him turn loose one of those big haw-haw-haws, but nothing fazed him. He looked ready to do murder."

116

"He's mad at the Native Son," Rena observed fatuously.

"You don't say so!" Len's shoulders twitched with impatience. Although Rena was a good girl and a loyal friend, her mental limitations sometimes palled on Len. But with the next breath she returned to her immediate worry. "What do you suppose has struck that soft-eyed Adonis all of a sudden?"

"If you mean Miguel—why, he certainly was as nice as pie."

"Pie!" Len gave another twitch of exasperation. "He was *deadly* sweet. He—scares me when he acts like that. He's up to something. Take Big Medicine and that pop-eyed glare of his, and Mig smiling and apologizing all over the place—and a devil way back in his eyes— oh, I wish to goodness they'd all come down with smallpox! Maybe that would take some of the fight out of them."

"Pock marks," said Rena gravely, "is terrible. You wouldn't want to see Bert—"

"Oh, shut up! Go on up and get Myrt out of bed, will you? Her lily fingers will have to get busy with the dishpan this morning, while you tackle this floor. One way to stave off a killing is to stuff those hyenas with pie and cake. You know the old song, Rena—

" '*Men are only boys grown tall;*
Hearts don't change much, after all.'

So it's up to us to keep them calmed down with good food. The Countess has got nothing on me—I'll make a chocolate cake right now. And Rena, if that lazy trollop doesn't crawl out and get to work here, douse her with cold water."

"If I tell her you called her a trollop, she'll come fast enough—but then look out!" giggled Rena.

"I could call her worse than that without stretching the truth much," Len retorted, with a grim look around her mouth. "Tell her the dishwater is boiling and her beaux are all flying up the chimney." With a last troubled glance toward the corrals, where riders were already mounting to bring in the horses and begin the work of the day, Len turned back to her self-imposed task of keeping the males of her species well fed and comfortable.

Len was not the only person to worry that morning over the Native Son's incredible amiability. More than once certain members of the Happy Family tilted hat crowns together in earnest private conferences, and in the intervals of bronk-riding puzzled eyes shot sidelong glances toward Miguel and afterwards sought other eyes in silent questioning.

Even Andy Green betrayed uneasiness. More than once during the forenoon his gray eyes rested upon the Native Son in troubled speculation, and when the dinner call came and they were straggling up the slope to the bunk-house he beckoned Miguel with a guarded tilt of the head. The two fell into step behind the others, and Miguel waited expectantly, smoking and watching Andy from the tail of his eye.

"Well, *amigo,* what's eating on you now?" he grinned.

"Well, you oughta know. You're too darned agreeable, Mig. What you been thinking of, to honey around Big Medicine the way you been doing all forenoon?"

"But I agreed to be friendly," drawled Miguel with a sardonic gleam in his eyes. "I promised to overlook—"

"When I told you to overlook anything he said or

118

done, I never thought you'd go it whole hawg. I asked you to treat him nice, but my Lord, I never expected you'd plaster compliments on him with a trowel."

"When I am good," said Miguel, "I am very, very good."

"Yeah, you're too good to live," snorted Andy. "And another thing: What'd you go and beller out Jones to Nameless, for? I thought that was to be kept just between us two."

"That," Miguel explained calmly, "was an experiment. It didn't work. Either that *hombre has* lost his memory just as he claims, or—well, a little romancing last night was perhaps needed, *amigo.*" He gave Andy a sudden penetrating look.

"Well, by gracious!" Andy's tone was deeply injured. "That's enough to make a man swear off on the truth for the rest of his life! If that guy ain't Larry Jones, I'll eat 'im raw!"

Whereupon the Native Son smiled a secretive, wise smile and diverged from the trail to the creek where the towels hung on bushes and cakes of soap were being hastily plucked out of a prune box set on the gravelly bank in the shade.

"Where yuh goin'?" Andy made suspicious demand.

"To change my shirt, *amigo.* And I think I shall shave now while the bunk-house is empty. I'm not hungry anyway."

"Off your feed, eh?" Andy gave him a quick, appraising glance. "Or maybe you're aiming to eat with the girls," he guessed shrewdly.

"*Quien sabe?*" replied the Native Son, falling back upon Spanish as he always did when he wished to be irritating or to be left alone.

Andy took the hint and went on about his business,

119

which took him to the creek. Savory odors, permeating the air in the immediate vicinity of the mess house as he passed, served to hasten his steps. Already a few of the boys were taking long steps toward their dinner, and the slower ones were splashing like mad, wanting to push their feet under the table as soon as any. Andy caught a cake of soap neatly in mid-air as Bert Rogers flung it toward the prune box and forgot everything but his appetite.

"Where's Mig?" Weary looked up from his dinner to question him as Andy straddled the bench beside him.

"Coming," said Andy, and surveyed the table hungrily before he reached for the roast beef.

Weary was satisfied for the time being. A little later, when the chocolate cake appeared and argument arose concerning the size of the pieces and the possibility of talking Len into making another just like it for supper, Weary forgot all about Miguel. It was Andy, leaning forward to look at Slim farther down on his side of the table, who noticed Big Medicine's empty place and took alarm.

"Bud, he didn't want no dinner," Slim explained in his heavy, deliberate way. "That gray he rode kinda shook him up and give 'im a headache, he said. He's went to lay down."

"Mig's in the bunk-house shaving," said Andy, getting up with the last of his wedge of cake in his hand. "Come on, Weary, we better go. Them two are liable to tangle."

"You said it," spoke up the pilgrim, whirling to his feet like a startled cat. "Big Medicine's been coiled and ready to strike ever since breakfast."

There was a loud scraping of feet on the floor, and the squawk of bench legs moved violently, but the pilgrim

120

was first outside, racing across to the bunk-house. At the door he stopped and listened, then shook his head in silent foreboding and went in, the others treading close on his heels.

Just at first they saw nothing at all save the big, crudely comfortable room with its beds and double-deck bunks neatly spread with their canvas tarps over the blankets. On one of them Big Medicine lay sprawling with his face to the wall. As the boys stood undecided, feeling rather foolish too, if the truth were known, he rolled over with a jerk and sat up, glaring at them with bloodshot eyes.

"Git outa here an' leave me be," he roared. "How many more's comin' to grin at me like a damned hyena? I'll lay yuh out, by cripes! I'll brain the next damn man that stands over me askin' kin he do anything! That (thus and so) greaser—"

"Where's Mig?"

Weary had advanced upon him, his face set in a terrible calm.

"In hell, where he b'longs!" growled Big Medicine, lying back heavily. "Can't come grinnin' over me—git outa here. I've stood all—all I'm a goin' to—sta-sta—stand."

Coming in out of bright sunlight as they had, the shadowed corners were blurred blotches of shade. But Pink, leaving the group at the door, had gone blinking to investigate the corners. Now he exclaimed sharply and dropped to his knees in the space between the stove and table.

"It's Mig. He's killed 'im!" Pink said in a tone of hushed horror.

"No!" Weary stooped, and between them they lifted the Native Son and laid him limp upon his bed.

121

"Knocked out, that's—" The words stuck in his throat. He stood staring stupidly at his own reddened palm and at the blood dripping from his little finger.

"—Stood enough, by cripes!" muttered Big Medicine, rolling glassy, bloodshot eyes vaguely toward the stunned group. Then he heaved his big body over on its side and lay with his face to the wall, mumbling incoherencies.

IT COULD HAVE BEEN A ROCK

THIS WAS BY NO MEANS THE FIRST TIME THE HAPPY Family had faced tragic emergencies. They bathed and bandaged the Native Son's head, their faces composed into a frozen calm that only betrayed the fear they hoped to hide. It was an ugly wound, evidently caused by striking the edge of the table with a good deal of force as he went down; which did not surprise any one, for Big Medicine always did strike a blow like a grizzly bear. It was clearly a case for a surgeon. Andy went up then and told J. G. that Mig had been thrown off a bronk and busted his head open on a rock and needed the doctor bad. Hadn't they better bring him up to the house? J. G. straightway damned all bronks and yelled to the Countess to get Chip and Dell's room ready for Mig-u-ell right away.

So they carried the Native Son up to the White House and put him to bed while Cal went up the trail to the flat rock and flagged the guards up on the hill, hurrying one off to town for help. And for the rest of that day an ominous quiet lay upon the ranch.

122

Once more the horses were turned out of the corral and hazed down into the lower pasture, since no one had the heart for riding. Before dark, Big Medicine was half led, half carried down to the hospital tent—for they were only too familiar now with certain premonitory symptoms. From his rambling talk they knew pretty well what had happened. What had looked to them like a glowering rage had been due mostly to the sickness he was fighting off as long as possible, until at noon he was forced to yield as his fever mounted. That was like Bud Welch, they gravely agreed. He wouldn't give in till the last minute, and he'd have died before he would say a word about how he felt, in the mood he was in after the fight.

The Native Son had gone into the bunk-house, no doubt still determined to be "very, very good." He had displayed altogether too much concern over Big Medicine, who hated to be guyed even when he was well. Miguel may have turned his back; he certainly must have been caught completely off guard when Big Medicine rose up and smashed him with the strength and fury born of growing delirium. Simple. Appallingly simple—and deadly.

Big Medicine lay muttering in the tent, with spells of shouting insane threats against the Native Son. Such times, three men were not too many to hold him in his bed, until the doctor came and rolled up Big Medicine's sleeve, pressed a tiny instrument against his arm with firm deliberation and rolled the sleeve down again. After that, two of the boys went off to bed for a few hours, leaving the other on guard at the bedside.

Up in the White House the Native Son lay still as a bronze statue, his heavy black lashes painting a deeper shadow on his tanned cheeks, his lips pressed together and showing the beginning of a smile at the corners. But

123

on his forehead, white where his silver-banded sombrero had kept off the sun, there lay a frown which gave to his whole face a troubled look of pain in spite of his half-smiling lips.

Hour after hour he had lain like that. The doctor came at dark, watched him for awhile with trained fingers on Miguel's quiet wrist; examined the wound on his head, readjusted the bandage and studied his face again.

"Been fighting, hasn't he?" He leaned and passed his fingers over some abrasions on Miguel's cheeks. "He could have got that injury in a fight—"

"There's been no trouble at all," J. G. told him testily. "It's hard on them boys, bein' penned in this coulee in round-up time. Winter, it wouldn't be so bad. They're always scufflin' and raisin' the devil, but there's been no fightin'. That was done on a rock. They been ridin' bronks."

"We-ell, it could have been a rock. Too bad you're all under quarantine here. This man should be in a hospital. If he lived to get there. As matters stand—"

Andy Green and Weary, listening outside the door, turned and tiptoed out to the porch. For half an hour they sat there dragging their boot-heels aimlessly along little trenches they had dug, but neither spoke a word. Their jaws were clamped tightly together and their eyes stared unseeingly at the ground.

Ages passed. Then the door behind them opened, flooding them with lamplight. They jumped to their feet and turned, searching the Old Man's haggard face. Pink, coming up from the tent, stood just outside the zone of light, listening. The Old Man did not say much. The doctor was doing all he could. Weary had better come inside where they could use him if necessary. Andy was to see that the message the Old Man held out to him was

124

sent off right away. Pink the Old Man did not see at all.

So Andy jumped on a horse standing saddled before the bunk-house, took the lantern Pink lighted for him and went galloping up the hill to the flat rock. There he waved and shouted until a guard rode down and dismounted at a safe distance. By the light of the lantern Andy read the message, which the guard wrote painstakingly in a notebook which he put away in his pocket.

"Mig must be pretty bad off," he remarked tentatively, reaching for the bridle reins. "Funny. I was watching that bronk-riding through my glasses. I never seen Mig throwed."

"That's the worst of them field glasses," Andy told him indifferently. "They don't show half that goes on." And he added, by way of a hint, "How long'll it take you to get that wire sent? Doc wants that surgeon to catch the 'leven-twenty outa Great Falls. That oughta put him here't the ranch before noon to-morra."

"Yeah, that's right. I'll take it in m'self. Say, I been wonderin' why none of us fellers seen you packin' Mig up from the corral. That's funny, 'cause—"

"Who said we packed him outa the corral? As it happens, Mig walked as far as the bunkhouse before he passed out. Nothin' funny about that, is there? And I'd hit for town if I was you and get that wire sent off. Wouldn't do any harm to give Gordon a coupla minutes to catch that train."

There was a certain menace in Andy's tone. The guard gathered up his reins and thrust his toe in the stirrup.

"Yeah, I'll hit the high spots, all right. Say, Bud's pretty bad too, ain't he?"

"Worst case we've had so far. You sure seem to keep

125

tabs on what goes on down our way," said Andy with grim irony. "Any other little thing you'd like to know, Ed, I'll tell yuh when you bring Doc Gordon down the hill. But if you're the cause of him missin' that train I'll just about kill yuh."

"Oh, all right, all right," Ed gruffly placated him as he swung to the saddle. "I got over four hours. Plenty time. You sure do manage to keep the road hot between here and town, I'll say that much."

"But don't say any more. *Ride!*"

The guard rode to some purpose. Well before noon a livery horse came tearing down the hill, and in the saddle, riding with the sureness of any cowboy on the range, came a tall, fair-haired Scot whose skill seemed greater to the Happy Family than the miracles of old. They did not go quite so far as to declare he could call the soul back into a dead body, but short of that, they were willing to back him in whatever he chose to do. They hailed him with subdued shouts of welcome and they grinned and reached for their sacks of Bull Durham while they watched him take the White House steps in one long springing stride. Over and over they assured one another that it was all right now. Nothing to worry about; Mig would be on his feet in no time. Doc Gordon was on the job.

For the rest of that day and through most of the night he remained on the job; so much so that the Happy Family grew long-faced and silent, sticking close to the bunk-house where they could see the doctor the minute he stepped outside. Only once did he leave the house and that was to make a hurried trip to the hospital tent in a cast-off suit of Weary's. The Happy Family—or the miserable few that were left unscathed—watched him go by without a word. In silence they waited for his

126

return and they tried to read his face as he hurried past them to the White House again. They were not the first to gaze anxiously into the inscrutable face of that great surgeon, gleaning no more than a vague hope that all would be well.

Then Weary came and dropped down on his heels beside them to snatch a smoke and give them what comfort he could.

"Bud's pretty sick," he said in the flat tone of repressed emotion. "I told Gordon the straight of it. I had to. You couldn't fool *him* with that rock story. He won't say anything, though."

"How's Mig?" Three voices uttered that question.

"Well—I don't know, boys. Gordon don't know himself. He's doing all that's humanly possible and he won't leave till he's satisfied—one way or the other." He smoked through a long and heavy silence, then roused himself and divulged certain gruesome details for their edification.

"Mamma, that man's sure a wizard! Know what he done? He took a little small dew-dad from his grip and went at Mig's head like he was working out his poll tax on a bad stretch of road. You know that long dent in his head? Mig's, I mean. Honest, boys, Gordon just cocked one eye down at Mig to see if he made a move, and he got busy like you'd pry a rock outa the ground. Lifted up a piece of skull darn near as wide as my two fingers. I was standin' right there with a towel over my face so I wouldn't breathe germs or anything onto Mig—and him living with smallpox under his nose for over two weeks!—and mamma! I could look right into Mig's head and see his brains!"

"Oh, shut up!" gasped Bert Rogers, looking sick.

"No, but honest! It wasn't so bad. He sure done a neat

job. And the way Gordon grinned when Mig opened his eyes and kinda walled them around (like a baby sizin' things up in a strange place), it's a cinch that was a good sign. But he passed out again right away and he ain't made a move since. Gordon says the next few hours oughta tell the tale."

"If he don't get over it," speculated the pilgrim, "our friend Big Medicine will be in all kinds of a fix."

"Not on your life," Weary stated firmly. "He wasn't responsible—and anyway, Mig got hurt ridin' a bronk. You don't want to overlook that fact, any of you; not in public, anyway. Gordon told me Bud has been sick longer than we had any idea of and that's what made him so mean and touchy. Packing Nameless in to the ranch was quite a strain on him and I guess Big Medicine has had pains and aches he never would own up to. Then this last deal, coming on top of everything else—Gordon said it was a wonder to him how Bud kept going all this while. The last day or so he was liable to do or say most anything."

"We don't need a doctor to tell us that," Andy put in with some bitterness.

"No, but we sure might need him to protect Big Medicine if—well, if Mig don't pull through." Weary looked gravely from one to the other. "We're all together here, the only ones that know just what took place. We ain't kids. We've always hung together when it came right to a showdown, and we will now. Bert, you're one of the bunch, even if you ain't on the Flying U payroll. And Nameless, you owe Big Medicine a debt you might be called on to pay before we're through. Gordon says, no matter what was the name of the object that caved in Mig's skull that way, he got that injury by accident. We stick to the story Andy told J. G."

128

"And what about Big Medicine, blatherin' the whole thing down there in the tent, right before Bing?" Pink demanded. "Old Patsy's all right, and so is Happy; but to tell you the truth, I don't go so much on Bing."

"Bud's plumb outa his head," Weary pointed out. "All he has said could apply to that fight we all got into. And when he gets over this," he added meaningly, "I sure hope he forgets all about it and that nobody'll ever tell him."

There was a silence made uneasy by their anxious thoughts.

"Oh, well," said Pink at last, with a forced cheerfulness, "No use crossing that bridge now. I'm as sure as that I'm setting here that it'll turn out all right." His glance strayed wistfully toward the house. "Nothing like that'll happen to our Native Son."

From the heart of every man there rose a silent amen.

THE NATIVE SON

ONE DAY IN THE MIDDLE OF JULY (TIME AND EVENTS having moved steadily forward as they have always done in obedience to cosmic law), a pathetically handsome shadow of the Native Son walked with the slow circumspection of a convalescent into the White House living room and asked the Little Doctor if she supposed Andy Green was anywhere around the place.

It happened to be early in the afternoon of a blistering Sunday. It was so hot the chickens wallowed low on their wishbones in the moist hollows they had scratched under the willows. On such a day no man was likely to exert himself more than was necessary, and the Little Doctor hoisted her

129

oldest umbrella and walked in the shade of it to fetch Andy from the bunk-house.

"And the rest of you boys better stay put," she advised in the pleasingly dictatorial tone which she assumed sometimes when it seemed best that earnestness should parade as a joke. "Miguel's enough of a job as it is. I'll have to hobble him to hold him any longer. He's been trying to break back into the herd ever since I let him put his boots on."

"Why don't yuh hog-tie 'im?" suggested Happy Jack, whose complexion was still somewhat mottled but whose nature remained unchanged by the ordeal he had come through.

"Well, he's got to learn to use his legs again sometime, you know. If you all behave yourselves and keep away from him except when you're invited, I'll maybe promote him to the bunk-house in a week or so. Come on, Andy. Miguel isn't the most patient man in the world."

So Andy took the old umbrella—two of its ribs thrust shamelessly out into the hot sunlight—and escorted the Little Doctor back to the house. And presently he and the Native Son were reclining at ease on a quilt spread under a cottonwood down by the creek behind the house, out of sight and hearing of every one on the ranch. One of the Little Doctor's biggest and softest sofa cushions was crushed behind the Native Son's head and shoulders, and even Andy was conscious of an odd thrill at the sheer beauty of Miguel's face, thinned by illness, and the wistful languor of his soft brown eyes shining between their heavy fringe of black curled lashes. Andy almost laughed aloud at the incongruity of Miguel's first words, they were so unlike the picture he made.

"Say, you aren't packing anything on your hip, are you, Andy?" He raised his mournful brown eyes for a hopeful glance. *"Dios!* I'd give my best boots for a quart of Metropole right now."

"You're darned lucky to be alive," Andy pointed out, smothering a laugh.

"If you call it living." Miguel's melodious voice was charged with sarcasm. "Milk three times a day, custard and coddled egg. Laying me cold with his six-gun is nothing to what I've got chalked up against Big Medicine for letting me in for all this granny grub they've been feeding me. *Dios!* I never want to see a cow again as long as I live. Milk toast!" The Native Son spat eloquently. "I'm afraid to open my mouth for fear I'll cackle. Sure there's no whisky on the ranch, *amigo?"*

"It's a cinch there ain't," Andy told him regretfully. "Nobody's been to town since the middle of the week. Happy brought out a bottle then, but it sure lasted quick. We had a hell of a drouth, remember. It'll take about all summer to get soaked up so we'll hold water again. Why, Slim run acrost the empty bottle last night and went to chewin' the cork. Nope, there ain't a drop on the ranch, you can bank on that."

"Baw-aw-aw!" groaned the Native Son in whimsical disgust. "Roll me a smoke then." Looking like a picture of the angel Gabriel, the Native Son lay back at languid ease until he might enjoy the forbidden luxury of a cigarette.

"What's going on, *amigo?"* With smoke ribboning out from his nostrils, Miguel looked less spiritual and much more natural. "This is the first time I've been let out of the corral, so I haven't had a chance to talk to any of you fellows. There's always been a woman somewhere within hearing. Little Red Loco has been faithful as—" He slanted a glance at Andy and blew three smoke rings from his smiling lips.

131

"Yeah, I heard about Myrt sticking right by you. I heard—is it a fact that you're engaged to Myrt?"

"Why do you ask that, *amigo?*"

"Because I wanted to find out," Andy retorted bluntly. "Myrt's been dropping hints lately."

"Little Red Loco has been very sweet."

"Yeah, I don't doubt that a minute." Looking at the Native Son lying back against the cherry satin of that cushion, Andy thought that any girl in the country would have been sweet to so handsome a patient. "Has she gone home for good? I noticed Bert took a couple of grips in the buggy last night when he come after her."

"I'm no longer in need of a nurse," Miguel said drily. "I'll soon be able to ride."

"Oh. Sure." With a dry twig Andy began absently to draw a map on the ground just beyond the quilt-edge.

"Before I'm turned back into the herd, I'd like to know what's been taking place around here. How about it, *amigo?* Has Nameless decided to remember his past yet?"

Andy chuckled and rolled over to prop himself on an elbow, facing the Native Son.

"Little things kinda come back to him now and then," he returned, grinning to himself. "Just enough to get along on. He's discovered that he's a pretty good runner, just lately. Him and Big Medicine ride off by themselves most every day for a workout, as he calls it. He never explained where he got hold of that term. They go off away from the ranch and then Nameless gets down and runs along on foot. Bud's been braggin' that Nameless can keep right at the tail of a horse on the lope for five miles."

"You believe that?"

"Well, I'd hate like sin to bet it wasn't so. Another

thing, Mig—I don't know as any of the boys have told you this—Nameless has glommed onto the name you gave him that last morning at breakfast. When you was so bad there awhile back, he kinda got a sentimental streak or something. He said you'd give him the name of Rufus Jones, and as long as he didn't have a name to go by, he was goin' to take that. When they raised the quarantine, him and Big Medicine rode in to Dry Lake one day to try and get a line on Nameless' pardner that died. 'Course, everything he had on him was burnt, and the fellow was buried away back up on the hill by himself and a bob-wire fence built around the grave. They said there wasn't a thing in his clothes to tell who he was or where he come from, so Nameless is Rufus Jones. Compliments of Mig Rapponi." Andy laughed. "Slick, what I mean."

"Me—or him?" asked the Native Son, forgetting his college training for the moment.

"Him," said Andy, who had never come within gunshot of a college. "He's playin' according to Hoyle, Mig. Framing to run against all comers on Labor Day, and taking the name of Jones like he's done, nobody's got any kick comin' afterwards if they get wise to who he is."

"Do the boys know yet?"

"They do not." Andy's mouth hardened a little. "You know how I tried to tell 'em, that night of the big settin'. Well, I just let it ride that way. They're building up a fine large time for Labor Day, with horse races, a prize fight and all the trimmings." He grinned. "Rufus Jones has entered for about every event, except maybe the horse race, and I ain't sure but what he'll go out for that, him against the field. Big Medicine sure is playin' him up strong. They've got boxin' gloves down in the bunkhouse, Mig, and the bunch is growin' cauliflower ears

133

a'ready, training with Nameless; or letting him paw 'em around to get himself in shape. And down in the saddle shed there's a punchin' bag that's about wore a hole in the roof. Some darn fool's always takin' a punch at it."

"Big Medicine, I suppose, goes after it with his gun," drawled the Native Son.

"No he don't—say, what gave you the idea that he— Mig, don't you know how you got hurt?" Andy sat up and crossed his legs Turk fashion. He could argue more fluently when both hands were free. "You said something awhile back about him using his six-gun. Mig, your head hit the table when you went down. That's how—"

"Was the table upset?"

"Well, no, but you probably steadied it with your body." Andy frowned and began rubbing the fire out of his cigarette against a rock.

"You know that couldn't happen. And if it could— listen to me, Andy Green. I had taken off my hat and was reaching up to that shelf for the shaving cup, and I was struck from behind; with a six-shooter, I think. Big Medicine hits like the kick of a mule, but that was no fist on my head, *amigo*. I've been knocked down before in my life. It was a gun. There are no blackjacks in the bunk-house." His smile was bitter. "It was meant to kill me and it nearly did."

Andy was sifting tobacco into a fresh cigarette paper, and some was spilled before he was through. Then he looked up, his gray eyes holding Miguel's gaze with impelling honesty.

"Bud was batty," he declared succinctly. "He was talkin' wild and scattering when we got there. You ask Weary what Doc Gordon said about it, if you don't want to take my word. He said Big Medicine wasn't

134

responsible for anything he said or done. And you know, Mig, I told yuh to go slow. You was sure runnin' him ragged with that politeness stunt you was pullin'. You can't hardly blame Bud, sick as he musta been, and all that."

"He knew what he wanted."

"What he thought he wanted at the time. And say, Mig, if you ain't satisfied—if you want to get back at Big Medicine—well, he got all that was coming to him, all right. Did Myrt tell you?"

"Tell me what? We can find pleasanter subjects than Big Medicine."

"Well, I sure thought somebody woulda told yuh." Andy peered doubtfully into his face. "Wait till you see him. Mig, if you thought he was a homely cuss before, you sure oughta see him now. His eyebrows are gone and his winkers, and he's as red as a gobbler's neck. His hair has just about all fell out, and honest, he's pitiful to look at. The Little Doctor says he'll improve with time, and his hair'll grow back in. But if you've got any quarrel with Big Medicine, forget it. That boy's had a plenty."

"But I didn't bring that to him. Why doesn't he take it out on Nameless?"

"Oh, well—" Andy flung out his hands in a vague gesture that yet implied a great deal "—you know Bud. He saved his life or thinks he did. And we all beefed around so much about it that he'd die before he'd make a holler. You oughta hear him go on now about Nameless as a boxer and a runner and a few other things. According to him, Nameless could step out and whip the world."

The Native Son sagged lower against the cushions. A tired, dreary look came into his face, as if he were remembering how quickly Big Medicine would have boasted about his fine qualities and achievements before the coming of this stranger. He bit his lip, but the question in his mind nevertheless forced itself into words.

"And what does he say—about me?"

"You?" Andy's glance flickered. A brown bird restlessly hopping from twig to twig on a wild cherry bush near by claimed his attention. "Well, you know how he is, Mig. Stubborn as a mule. He's sorry as hell, but—"

"What does he say?"

"Not a word. From the time the fever left him and he quit raving, I don't believe he's mentioned your name once. When us boys talk about you, Big Medicine listens—I've seen him hold a cigarette halfway to his mouth for a minute or more, Mig, when somebody spoke about how you're gettin' along. But not a yelp outa him. You can tell by his face, though, and his eyes. Even when some of the boys got to talkin' about you and Myrt being engaged, he never had a word to say about it, one way or the other. Nameless did. Nameless grinned and said he wished you much joy."

"Half of Big Medicine's grudge against me was jealousy," Miguel recalled, as one does who broods upon past wrongs.

"Well, he's give that up, I guess. He kinda shied off from Myrt after he got well. By gracious, I don't blame him! I would too, if I looked the way he does. But Myrt was awful nice to him, I'll say that for her. Uh course, nothing you'd need to mind," Andy hastily interposed. "Just nice and thoughtful, wanting to make him feel good. And that musta took nerve. Man, oh, man, but he's sure a hard looker!"

The Native Son's expression did not change, though Andy watched for it. His eyes were somber, his mouth unsmiling. He stirred finally, pulled a cushion higher behind his shoulders, reached out his hand for the cigarette Andy was on the point of offering.

"So a few things are clear to me now," he said slowly, exhaling smoke through his nostrils. "Loping Larry is still just Nameless, except that to outsiders he is Rufus Jones. You think even Big Medicine isn't wise!"

"I know he ain't, Mig."

"So he is a real dark horse. That will be interesting, *amigo*, to watch how he does it."

"My money'll be on him; every nickel I can rake and scrape between now and Labor Day. In Minot I was one of the suckers that bet against him. Lord-ee, how that boy can run!"

"And so the boys have all accepted my engagement—"

"Yeah, they kinda smelled a mouse when the quarantine was lifted and still Myrt didn't want to leave but insisted on staying to help nurse you. Some of the boys said then that Myrt had really fell for your fatal beauty. And lately, when we kinda teased her about it, she didn't do a thing but admit it. When's it to be, Mig?"

"Do I look like getting married?" Miguel turned a reproachful glance upon Andy. "Be sure of one thing, *amigo*; when we have set the wedding day, you will be the first to know about it from me."

"Well," Andy said with dubious optimism, "I guess you're old enough to pick the wife you want, Mig. Myrt seems to be turning out better'n a fellow'd expect. She sure has settled down a lot since you've been hurt. The Little Doctor told Weary she didn't know what she'd of done without Myrtle. I guess—" Andy forced a higher

137

degree of sprightliness "—if you're crazy enough to tie yourself up to any woman for life, Myrt'll make a right nice little wife. The bunch'll miss yuh like the devil, Mig, but we all wish yuh well—and all kinds of luck."

"All kinds," murmured the Native Son. "So far I've been getting it, I think. And Nameless—has the announcement spoiled that friendship?"

"Him and Myrt, you mean? Well, he's kinda cooled off; it was up to him to back down, I reckon. But they're friendly—sure they are. He took his medicine like he always does, laughing and kidding Myrt. He sure is an amiable cuss. All the deviling he's had from the bunch, he's never once got upon his hind legs and made any kinda war talk. And he could mop the earth with any one of us. No, him and Myrt are just friendly and no more. Like all the rest of us, Mig. You ain't got a rival in the world that I know of." He hesitated, eyeing the Native Son surreptitiously. "When did you say you two was aiming to get spliced?"

"*Quien sabe?*"

"All right, darn yuh, don't tell if you don't want to. But just remember, Mig, I'm about the best friend you've got in the world and I've got your interests at heart. You meant it, didn't yuh, what you said about my being the first one you'd tell?" Andy's laugh could not hide the earnestness beneath it.

"All that—and more."

Miguel's long lashes drooped, sleep-weighted. Andy's mouth, opened for speech, closed in silence. He sat back on his heels and watched while Miguel took two long winks, forgetting to open his eyes after the last one. The lashes lay black and thick upon his cheeks where the deep tan had lightened to the pallor of long illness. The half-smoked cigarette slid from his lax fingers to the quilt. Andy leaned and picked it up, rose very slowly and went away, walking on his toes.

When he was gone the Native Son opened his eyes and lay staring into the branches over his head. "Friendship!" he gritted in a savage whisper. "He never once speaks my name—not even to ask if I will live or die. Friendship!"

Until the Little Doctor came to call him, he lay there staring with the fixed, unseeing gaze of a dead man up into the branches; thinking, thinking—with his handsome mouth set in the bitter lines of poignant memory and his eyes clouded with trouble.

RUFUS RECALLS SOMETHING

GRASS AND WEEDS ALREADY GREW WHERE THE hospital tent had disappeared in flame on the last day of June, and only the brighter patch of green and the bare flagpole marked the spot where it had stood. Had the guards who rode along the coulee's rim with loaded rifles tied to their saddles looked down upon the familiar scene in the latter part of August, they would have observed a ranch apparently wrapped in the peace of a well-ordered existence. They would have seen the Happy Family ride out in the coolest hour of morning, scattering to their various tasks of the day, and they would have seen them loitering in the grateful shade of bunk-house or stable during their hours of leisure.

They would have seen Rufus Jones go trotting up over the hill in the dawn, running like a lone wolf where the land lay emptiest, and they would have seen him wrestling like a playful pup on the stretched canvas down beside the saddle shed, and heard the shouted advice and jeering criticisms when his training partner flopped with monotonous regularity upon his back and stayed until he was released. They would have heard whoops of laughter, loud bantering, the indistinguishable clamor of good-natured argument. They would have ridden away, half-enviously thinking that the Flying U sure was about the happiest ranch in the country and that the boys who called it home hadn't a care in the world.

On a certain sultry afternoon the deceptive air of friendliness and perfect peace was more than usually apparent. It happened that Chip and the Little Doctor had driven home from Dry Lake not more than an hour before, and the Happy Family, having made a short day of their work, were lounging in the shade as they loved to do, when Chip came down from the house for a visit.

"Looks to me, Rufus, like a fine large day for you when you go after those purses they're hanging up in town," he began at once, with a quizzical twinkle in his eyes. "They've boosted 'em another notch. Have you heard the latest?"

"I don't know—Bert Rogers was telling me yesterday that a Swede up at a town they call Shelby has got a notion he can wrestle. He's coming down to show us. Hear anything more?"

"I'd tell a man! He's a holy terror, they say. He laid 'em all on the mat in Kalispel the Fourth."

"*Haw-haw-haw-w-w!*" chortled Big Medicine. "Let 'im come! Let 'em *all* come! By cripes, I'll bet my next six months' wages awn Rufus here, ag'inst all the Swedes in the country!"

"I wouldn't be too previous with my hard-earned coin, if I were you, Bud," Chip warned. "The worst is yet to come. A couple of those Milk River outfits have thrown in together and entered that Spokane athlete,

Red Willis. He's been cleaning up on the Coast lately. One of the Four-Eleven boys is a cousin of his and he got Red to promise he'd come if they'd make it worth his while. All the Northern outfits are backing him to the hilt."

"The more the merrier," Nameless quoted equably.

"By golly, they got no right to ring in professionals!" Slim protested loudly. "That's agin the rules! Nameless don't have to go up ag'inst Red Willis and I'll tell 'em so."

"What's Dry Lake going to do about it?" Weary wanted to know. "Fifty dollars ain't any inducement to a man like Red."

"And don't think Dry Lake isn't wise to that fact." Chip looked up from tearing an infinitesimal strip from a cigarette paper; the brown kind. "Somebody pointed out to our leading citizens that a crowd of outsiders will bring money into the town and make up for what it lost last spring during the smallpox scare. There was a public meeting held Saturday night in the schoolhouse and Dry Lake decided to do itself proud. I brought a revised list of events and purses, if any one's interested." His drawl emphasized the irony of the last phrase.

"If they go t' work and change everything around and ring in champeens on us, all bets is off and I'll tell 'em so," Slim declared, his worried gaze going to the paper and then to Nameless, who was reading it with Big Medicine, Cal and Pink looking over his shoulder. "They needn't think they can run any such a rannigan on me, by golly. I wouldn't stand for it a holy minute, Nameless. What you better do is ride in there and tell 'em where they get off at."

"Only somehow I don't care how many champs they

run in on me. I may not be so good, but I'm willing to bet I can give 'em a run for their money. Who is this Red Willis, anyhow?"

With much elaboration they told him, and their distaste for Red's presence on Labor Day increased with every victory of his that they recalled. They did not belittle his achievements, and Nameless listened with a half smile. Moreover, they told him just why the boys up on Milk River would give the shirt off their backs for a chance to ride home with good Flying U dollars jingling in their pockets. It had to do with the last horse races held at Malta, the year before.

"Yeah, them geezers from Milk River has been waitin' for a chance to git back at us," Slim put in. "We rode in there and cleaned the crowd." He thereupon repeated all the intricate details of the cleaning process, and even enumerated the luxuries indulged in afterwards by the Happy Family during an orgy of buying leather goods displayed in the latest Sears Roebuck catalogue.

To all of this and more did Nameless listen and still his face showed no concern. For the third time he read the rules officially adopted by the committee on sports and laughed as he handed the paper back to Chip.

"Fine and dandy. It's free for all and that suits me fine. Of course," he modestly conceded, "this Spokane lad may be all he's cracked up to be and he may beat me to a frazzle. Still—I'll take a chance if you fellows will. That hundred-yard dash looks good to me. Go light on the wrestling and back me as hard as you can on that foot race. That's my advice."

"Oh, we're backing yuh," Pink told him a bit grudgingly. "But you must admit that Red Willis kinda puts a different face on things. And it ain't the money that counts the most from now on, either. We've got to beat Milk River or we'll have to wade in afterwards and clean up the whole outfit. I know them Northern boys from away back. You've sure got your work cut out for yuh, Nameless."

"Say," demanded Big Medicine, "where'd you git the idee that Nameless is liable to lose out? Little One, if I didn't know you're good at heart I'd shore lose my temper with you. Nameless 'll win at a walk. Shore he will!" His hand came down on the pilgrim's shoulder in an affectionate slap that would have sent some men sprawling.

"He will—if Red Willis would kindly break a leg between now and Labor Day," Pink retorted glumly. "That's all right, Bud; I'm loyal as hell. But I sure do know that Milk River bunch and how they'll throw it into the Flying U outfit if their man wins. Nameless is good—"

"Shore he's good! There ain't nobody kin touch 'im," Big Medicine reiterated jealously.

"Too bad he can't remember where he learned his stuff," Andy hinted, glancing surreptitiously across at the Native Son.

"Yeah, I sure wish I could," Nameless regretfully agreed. "All I can say is, I feel awful confident. When I'm running it's just as if I've done it all before, but where or when—" He shook his head with a look of bafflement.

"By cripes, it don't make no difference at all," Big Medicine declared, with a challenging look around. "You can run and you can wrassle. I'll back yuh agin all comers, whether the rest will or not."

His glare chanced to fall upon the Native Son, whose left lid was at that precise instant wrinkling to a wink that answered Andy Green's signal of amused understanding. Big Medicine's face froze to a look of cold ferocity. His teeth came together with a snap that lumped the muscles along his jaw. For the time it would take to count ten they stared into each other's eyes, soul speaking to soul in the wordless language that sears deeper than speech.

Big Medicine's eyes were the first to flicker and turn away. The Native Son lifted his shoulders in the shrug that could mean so much or so little. With infinite calm he pushed the ash from his cigarette with a negligent finger which supported a ring with a large round moonstone setting, turned and sauntered down toward the corrals. It was significant that no one called after him or gave any sign. The Happy Family were holding themselves to a rigid neutrality that did not permit so much as a glance of recognition. But presently Andy also detached himself from the group and followed.

Miguel was standing by the corral gate, one hand upon the chain. But he had made no move to unhook its fastening. He was bowed forward, his forehead resting against his wrist. "It's me, Mig," Andy announced himself softly, when his footsteps brought Miguel up with a start.

"And what do you want?" The Native Son's voice was coldly defensive.

"Oh, nothing. Just got tired of all that chin-whackin' up there." He waited for a minute. "What's the matter? If yuh don't feel good—"

"I'm all right. You know what it is. I'm going away. If I don't—" Miguel's teeth ground together with an audible sound. And suddenly all the cold repression of the weeks just past gave way before a tumult of words.

"Why does he hate me so? You tell me he is sorry,

144

but if looks could kill—And we were friends. No matter if we did torment each other and quarrel now and then, we were like brothers. Under all the joshing and the hard words we were friends. I would fight for him—A man doesn't talk of those things, but we know. All of us against the world, if that is how it comes. *Compadres*. Pals. And why—You say he is sorry. You say it eats into his heart that he came so close to killing me—

"I would forgive that, because I was very much to blame. I said the things I knew would hurt the most. But not to make any man do murder. Not to make him hate me more because he failed to kill. When I came down among you again, it was as if I did not exist. One look he gave me and turned away his face. Not one word has he spoken—"

"Yeah, and not a word have you said to him, Mig. You got to see his side too." Andy hesitated, choosing his words with care. "Up there, just now—I saw the whole play. You and me was giving each other the wink, you remember, on account of what we know about Nameless. Big Medicine, he's kinda hot under the collar because it looks like the bunch is beginning to get cold feet. He's declared himself and looks around to see what effect he's having; and what does he see but you, giving me the wink.

"Figure it out yourself, Mig. Wouldn't you have thought it was on you—puttin' yourself in Bud's place? And that ain't the first time you've got each other wrong." Andy's forehead was drawn into three deep wrinkles between his eyes. "If you two could get together and thrash it out—"

"It would be with guns. No other way. And I have taken his black looks—or no looks at all, which is worse—because a little while ago he was my friend. But I warn you, *amigo*, I had better go now, before the shooting begins."

145

"Ah, forget it, Mig! Stay and clean up a wad of money before yuh go, anyway. Gosh, we can't allow any strayin' away from the herd now, doggone yuh! We'll need you to help set that Milk River crowd in their places. You wouldn't throw us down now, would you? Even with Bert and Bing and Joe Meeker, they'll be almost two to one. Of course," he artfully conceded, "no one can stop you, if you're dead set on going, but it sure wouldn't set very well with the boys to have one of us crawl out right at the last minute. We've always been kinda accustomed to hangin' together. And if we had any little hard feelings amongst ourselves, we sure didn't peddle the news to outsiders. We kept it private and turned a solid front to the world."

The Native Son was exceedingly busy at that moment, pulling a splinter off the rail he leaned his shoulder against. His big hat shielded his face from view and he neither looked up nor made any reply, though Andy waited for a full minute.

"Of course," he repeated his most cutting remark, "no one can stop you. You're a free moral agent and you'll do as you damn' please. If your own personal feelings means more to yuh than the reputation this outfit's got for sticking together, go ahead. Irish," he added with caustic emphasis, "is comin' on the run. He wrote Chip he'd be here by next Sunday, with every dollar he could beg, borrow or steal, and he'd bet on our man sight unseen. He said he had some friends that are pretty good scrappers and he'll try and bring 'em along so as to insure a square deal for our man. And that," he made biting comment, "is what we call sticking together. But of course—"

He got no further, for Miguel was cursing him in two languages and his vocabulary was not limited in either. Andy was grinning from ear to ear when a great clamor

146

arose at the bunk-house. From the sounds, the Happy Family had suddenly become uproariously drunk or they were already celebrating some unbelievable victory. Andy's fingers clamped down on the Native Son's arm.

"You tell me the rest some other time, Mig. Let's go see what all's happened up there."

"But if you ever again so much as hint to me that I am capable of disloyalty—"

"Forget it, Mig, and come on! Holy smoke, would yuh listen to that!"

As they neared the corner of the shed, the tumult roared around it, sweeping them back with the resistless push of an ocean roller. Yip-yipping like a war party of Sioux, the Happy Family bore Nameless aloft upon their shoulders. Snatches of sentences detached themselves from the clamor.

"Hey, Mig! Andy! Rufus got to huntin' around—"

"Boys! Lookit what Nameless—"

"Bring on your champs, by golly!"

"Calm down, you hyenas! Let Nameless—"

"Rufus, you tell 'em!"

They stood the pilgrim upon his own feet, shoved him forward to face Andy and Miguel and hushed their noise that they might drink in with avid interest the incredible story he had to tell.

LOPING LARRY JONES

WITH HIS FACE AGLOW AND HIS IRISH EYES DANCING with excitement, Nameless stood waving before their astonished faces a full page torn from an old magazine published in California—if the printed line at the top meant anything. In the center of the wrinkled and

147

weather-stained sheet a large and rather well done picture stared out at them. The figure was clad in running trunks and bore a startling resemblance to himself.

"I was hunting a gold pencil that was in my grip," he explained breathlessly. "The darn thing slid to the bottom and I was feeling around for it when it slipped through a lining I never noticed before. I was feeling in there after it and I pulled out *this!*"

"Well, whadda-yuh-know-about-that!" exclaimed Andy, nudging the Native Son with his elbow, as his fingers closed upon the proffered paper.

"It all come back to me in a flash, soon as I looked at that picture of me," Nameless cried eagerly. "Larry Jones—yuh know," he interrupted himself to send an inclusive glance around the group. "I thought it was kinda funny, the feeling that come over me when Mig said Jones was a good name for me. It's a fact, I felt goose-pimply for a minute. *Larry Jones.*" He savored the name with mind and tongue. "Loping Larry, they called me—it's there in that piece. I remember it now."

"No!" cried Andy again, in the tone a good elocution teacher would use to illustrate astonishment.

"I sure do. Of course," Nameless hedged cautiously, "it ain't *all* clear to me. What that piece says I know is true, but I can't seem to remember everything—"

"Remember runnin' a race three years ago in Minot, South Dakota?" Andy's steady gray eyes watched him unblinkingly.

"Why—no, I don't." Loping Larry's eyes were as wide-open and as honest as Andy Green's.

"I kinda thought you wouldn't," Andy told him gently.

"We've got to keep this quiet," Pink insisted. "If a

word of this leaks out so that Milk River bunch gets hold of it—"

"Oh, mamma!" sighed Weary, visioning disaster.

"No reason why it should leak out," Chip stated definitely. "They've got their champ corralled and we've got ours. It's a stand-off and they can't holler if they get trimmed."

Pink, having been jostled in the excitement, found himself standing alongside Andy Green. In the center of the group Big Medicine was vociferously proclaiming his sentiments to the world and Pink chanced to observe a peculiar look of secret mirth on Andy's face.

"Say, don't you realize what this means to us?" Pink demanded in a reproachful voice. "Read that record over again."

"No, I don't have to," Andy refused, vainly trying to pull his twitching mouth straight.

"Well, what're you grinning so sarcastic about?" challenged Pink. "Look at that picture. Loping Larry Jones. Ain't it the dead image of Nameless?"

"Sure, it is," Andy admitted, with another secret nudge for the Native Son.

"Well, damn it, wipe off that grin!" Pink's eyes were stormy.

"Who, me? I'm waitin' till I win back that forty dollars I lost on Loping Larry in Minot, three years ago," Andy drawled.

"*Lost* on him? Nameless?"

"I wanta tell yuh I did!" Andy handed back the paper with the weary air of a man whose wisdom goes far, far beyond his fellows and is therefore useless for his immediate purpose. It pleased him to see the abrupt change in the faces of the Happy Family.

"It's darned funny," snarled Pink, "that this is the first we've heard of it."

"Well," Andy was taking his time and enjoying every second of it, "that was what I kept trying to tell you boneheads away back in the middle of May. Mig and I have been wise to him all the time. I tried my best, but no, you smart Alecks thought you knew it all and then some."

"Aw, gwan!" growled Happy Jack. "I betcha you never knowed a thing about 'im, any more'n what we did. Ain't that right, Mig?"

"On the evening before—I fell off a horse and hit my head on a rock," said Miguel deliberately, "while we were taking a ride together, Andy told me how he lost forty dollars on the foot race in Minot, three years ago. He said that Nameless is Loping Larry. He remembered by the whistling." His languid gaze went around the group, flicking Big Medicine's face with a glance that stung. "He asks me to say nothing. I have my little joke next morning with the name, and we laugh together because we have a secret. Then I have—the accident. I have not told, because it is Andy's secret joke. And me—I do not betray my friend." He looked full at Big Medicine, whose face turned a deep magenta shade. "As to the money—"

"By gracious, it's a fact," Andy broke in. "I sure did lose money on that race. For-ty dollars. Just like that. I oughta know."

"Why, damn your picture," Nameless shouted in a sudden betraying fury, "that's a lie and I can prove it! I *won* that race in Minot. At a walk. I—"

"Oh," said Andy, grinning delightedly. "It's comin' back to yuh, is it?"

"When you say Minot, I—I kinda remember winning

150

a race there." Nameless stepped back, drawing his hand slowly across his eyes. "I *know* I won."

"Why, sure you won." Andy looked innocently around at the blank faces of the Happy Family. "To my sorrow. I was drunk as a boiled owl that day. I lost forty dollars bettin' on the other fella."

"*Haw-haw-haw-w-w!*" bellowed Big Medicine, moving aside so that his face was hidden from the Native Son. "Bettin' agin Loping Larry is jest throwin' money away. I told yuh all the time—"

"What we won't do to that Milk River bunch!" dimpled Pink "You know, Larry—"

"Say, can that Larry stuff," Nameless protested earnestly. "I'm Rufus Jones or Nameless—either one. But don't stub your toe, anybody, and call me Larry. Wouldn't you say so, Chip?"

"I certainly would. That outfit up north is importing the present champion on the Coast, which is stretching a point so fine the Labor Day committee had to get busy and frame new rules to let him in. They're turning an amateur sport into a money-making performance, because they know Red Willis will draw a crowd down from Benton and Havre—and even Great Falls is going to be represented, they tell me. So—"

"They'd come a heap farther and a darn sight faster to see Loping Larry," Big Medicine could not refrain from boasting at the top of his voice.

"Only they don't know it," Weary pointed out. "You'll have to tie a saddle string around Bud's nose so he won't whinny and give us all away," he added soberly.

"Shore is a lucky deal for us," Slim declared with ponderous emphasis, as if he had just that instant discovered the fact. "We got t' keep it dark, by golly."

"Well," said Pink, his dimples standing deep in both cheeks, "now you mention it, Slim, I believe it would be a good idea."

"They're pretty sure to get wise when they see him," Weary told them. "Didn't you ever go up against Red Willis, Rufus?"

"I—don't know. It doesn't mention him in that piece, does it?" Nameless looked distressed. "It's a darn shame, boys. I wish I could remember everything, but it seems as though the best I can do is—well, recognize a fact when it's pointed out to me. It's like trying to remember a name you've forgotten. You know—you rack your brain and it just won't come. You think till you're black in the face and then somebody says it for you and—well, there it is. You could kick yourself for not knowing it all the time. Red Willis sounds awful familiar, somehow, but all I get outa the name is a feeling that I ain't the least bit worried over him. I feel like it's a cinch in the hundred-yard dash. When it comes to wrestling, though—well, I don't feel quite so sure about it. I've kinda got a hunch I'll have my work cut out for me. That man Red Willis—"

"Well, here. Let's figure this thing out," Chip proposed, squatting down on his heels with the article on the ground and the butt end of a dried weed in his fingers. With a scrape of his palm he smoothed a place in the dust and poised his weed like a pencil.

"Red Willis has been in the game about five years, hasn't he? Mig, you came from the Coast—" Chip pushed back his gray hat and looked up.

"Willis was just beginning to be talked about when I left," said the Native Son, moving aside to be farther from Big Medicine before he went down on one knee beside Chip. "That was nearly six years ago. Some time

152

I spent in Arizona and Wyoming before I came here."

"Six years ago, Rufus, you were maybe matched against him somewhere. Can't you remember anything back that far?"

"No, I'm afraid I can't," said Nameless. "Let's see that piece again. This might be that old, don't you think? But there's nothing about Red Willis in it. According to this, I was some punkins at one time, and Mig says Red was making a name for himself too. There ought to be some mention of him here." He tossed the page down in front of Chip and got to his feet as if he were tired of the discussion. "What's the diff?" he cried impatiently. "Six years ago ain't now. Athletes break fast, sometimes. If he was such a much he wouldn't come to Dry Lake to settle the hash of some hick, not even if his cousin did ask it as a favor."

"His record—" began Chip, but Nameless interrupted him with a shade of arrogance.

"Well, *my* record ain't to be sneezed at, either. You've got it there in black and white. If that ain't good enough, I'll back down from the whole darn works. You've found out who I am. Now you can suit yourselves."

It suited the Happy Family to bet every two-bit piece they had in the world on Rufus Jones. That old write-up of Loping Larry was read into rags. Even Slim the slow-witted had conned it so often that he could—and did—repeat entire paragraphs of unstinted adulation. Irish, that turbulent cousin of Weary's who looked enough like him to be his twin, and whose entire mental make-up denied the physical likeness, came galloping in great haste to the ranch, curious to know what dark horse was concealed there.

Irish brought news from across the big river. Most of

153

the boys over on the Shonkin and the Musselshell were coming, he reported. News of Red Willis and the Swede from Shelby had spread into the most remote ranges. It was going to be a wonderful chance to see those two in action without having to pay for admission, and while he had heard some mild speculation concerning the man said to be entered by the Flying U outfit, without a doubt those other two were the big drawing cards. The kernel of his talk was what interested the Happy Family, however. Dry Lake would have the biggest crowd in its range history.

The days seemed to fly in a flock. Pink (who as every one knew hailed from the Northern ranges and had even been known as Milk River Pink until the name dropped from him at the Flying U) sent offensive challenging messages to the Four Eleven boys and hoped they would be repeated to other outfits. Which they were, with embellishments that would have pleased Pink enormously if he had heard them.

Nameless walked with a more perceptible swing to his shoulders, a more pantherish freedom in his hips. More than ever his head held its haughty poise of conscious superiority, his eyes looked out upon his world with cool indifference to any opinion save his own. Big Medicine's abject worship he took as his common right and the open admiration of the rest of the Happy Family he received with careless condescension.

He took no orders from any man and advice he waved aside as the meddlesome enthusiasm of the amateur. Loping Larry Jones would have the Happy Family understand that he knew the athletic game as they knew the trail from bunk-house to corral. According to that magazine article, he was the only consistent ten-second sprinter in America—or he had been at the time the

154

article was written. He could be depended upon to high-jump within a fraction of an inch of six feet, and it had taken the middleweight champion wrestler of America to put him three points down that season. For almost a year he had held the broad-jump record, but it was as a sprinter that he was expected to make a shining mark in the athletic world.

In other words, Loping Larry Jones was so good that it would have been foolish for him to pretend a diffidence in recognizing his goodness. Or so it apparently seemed to him.

Suddenly he displayed temperamental moods. It got his goat to have Big Medicine always tagging him whenever he left the coulee for a workout on the road. No need to hold a watch on him any more—they all knew what time he was making. Hell, didn't that piece say he was the most consistent sprinter in the game? He could train better alone. He seemed to remember that it always did make him nervous to have some darn trainer grannying around after him.

So when he pulled on his trunks in the gray dawn and laced his spike shoes which Chip had got for him, Nameless was free from espionage, however friendly it might be. He had a favorite stretch of road running west across the prairie for exactly six miles before it dipped into a thickly wooded draw, and up the hill and along this level stretch he would trot each morning, coming in to his training breakfast of toast, soft-boiled eggs and milk long after the boys had eaten and gone about their work.

One morning less than a week before Labor Day he failed to appear at his usual time, and Big Medicine, worried as a young mother whose child has run away, rode up to see what was the matter. In a remarkably short time he rode home again, glum and spiritless; but all he would say was that Nameless was all right. The Happy Family wondered, but they were wise enough to keep their conjectures to themselves until Loping Larry came trotting down the hill like a wolf coming late home from the hunt.

"Gittin' swelled head," grumbled Slim, who hated to see Big Medicine snubbed by his idol.

"Well, it ain't his head we're bettin' on; it's his heels," Cal told him philosophically. "Champs is always stuck on theirselves. You never seen any that wasn't."

"Yeah," grinned Andy, who had overheard the dialogue. "Don't let that bother yuh, Slim. Rufus is only actin' normal. There ain't a thing in the world to worry about. What I've seen of his workouts is better than he was on the track in Minot three years ago. He ain't lost a thing, far as I can see. After it's all over and the dust settles, you'll have more money than you ever saw in your life."

"Well, by golly, Bud wouldn't stand fer it in anybody else. Lookit the way he treats Mig, here. And then he lets Nameless treat him like a dog," Slim growled, unappeased. "By golly, I c'n hardly keep from takin' a crack at him myself, the way he cold-shoulders Bud half the time."

"Yeah, he does act like Big Medicine was his hired man that wasn't worth his wages," Andy cheerfully admitted. "But you want to recollect that Bud brought it on himself. I've always noticed that if yuh lay down and play doormat, some darn chump 'll wipe his feet on yuh, sure as the world. You can't blame Nameless, when Big Medicine has wrote welcome all over himself." He lifted his hat to cool his forehead, then waved toward the temporary, open-air gym which Nameless had ordered set up under the cottonwood where the hospital tent had stood last spring.

"Look at him go over that bar, would yuh! Wings sure wouldn't be any advantage to that bird."

"Nevertheless, that bird will need to fly," declared the Native Son, who had just ridden in from a visit to the Rogers ranch—his little patch of red *loco*, he called the place where Myrtle still lingered. "Bert was talking with a rider from up near Havre. They're claiming up on Milk River that Red Willis is doing his sprinting at ten seconds and less. He's at the Four Eleven now, training for the race. Rufus will not let any one see him run, lately. I do not understand that bird of yours, *amigo*." He looked at Andy across the back of his horse as he loosened the cinch. "One cannot have a honeymoon without money and my *dinero* is all of it fastened to the heels of our dark horse."

"He'll come loping home with it, Mig; don't you fret."

The Native Son lifted off saddle and blanket together and turned with them toward the shed.

"*Quien sabe?*" he flung back over his shoulder. "I should very much like to see that hombre sprint in earnest."

"You wait," said Andy sententiously. "You will, all right."

Thus, for not the first time in his unregenerate life Andy Green rose to the high plane of prophecy.

157

LEN LEARNS SEVERAL THINGS

THE PROPRIETOR OF THE PALACE HOTEL IN DRY LAKE was a canny soul who realized that, while crowds might once or twice a year fill his hostelry until the walls bulged outward, any real and lasting prosperity depended upon the friendship of his neighbors. Come who would to clamor for meals and lodging, always one table in his big square dining room was reserved for local guests. And at the end of the long narrow hall which divided the second story into two equal parts, six rooms were set apart for those who came in from the ranches on dance nights or for celebrations such as this particular Labor Day would furnish. Came they early or came they late, the women were sure of a room to rest in and to dress in their best; to leave wraps and parcels and to snatch a little sleep when the festivities were over and they must await the pleasure of their escorts who were likely to linger awhile in Rusty Brown's Elkhorn saloon across the way before they left for home.

For that reason the Palace Hotel was accepted as headquarters for all range dwellers when they came to town, and that is why Len Adams stood before the walnut-stained dresser in a room at the end of the hall, heating her curling irons by the somewhat primitive process of hanging them down the chimney of a bedroom lamp. Rena Jackson and the other women had already gone up to find seats in the makeshift grandstand built against the farther side of the stockyards fence, facing the level stretch of road down alongside the railroad track where the races would all be run. Rena had loyally offered to wait, but Len had shooed her off with the others so that Rena could save a place for her; or so Len said. It is possible that Bert Rogers, who still lingered in the Palace barroom, had something to do with the arrangement, however.

Certainly he was the unconscious cause of Len's last-minute decision to do her hair a different way. She had slept in a new kind of kid curlers the night before, and now she was not at all satisfied with the frizzes across her head. She looked like a topknot hen, she said. Even if she missed the potato race and the fat man's race it didn't matter. She simply was not going to show up in public with her hair like that. So here she was at the last minute heating her curling irons.

By turning her head toward the window she could watch all that went on in the street below. There wasn't much passing now. Nearly every one had already gone up to the stockyards, visible over the roof of Rusty Brown's Elkhorn saloon. If she tilted her head and looked sidewise to the left, she could see the general store up beside the railroad track, and if she craned in the opposite direction she could glimpse the front of the blacksmith shop at the other end of the street, and all of the front and side of the livery stable opposite. She therefore commanded a view of the entire town of Dry Lake with the exception of the schoolhouse and a few small dwellings behind the hotel. Bert Rogers had not left the barroom below; she was absolutely certain of that, because his horse Flopper was tied to the hitch rail beneath her window. He was going to run Flopper later in the afternoon in the saddle-horse race, so her deduction was fairly accurate. The Happy Family had left Rusty's place and ridden up to the stockyards some time ago. She would have wondered why Bert did not go with them, except that away down in her heart she knew well enough why. It was the same reason almost that she had for doing her hair a different way at the very last minute.

As she turned from the window to test the curling iron with moistened finger tip, she heard footsteps coming up the stairs. Not Bert's, of course; and no other man's steps mattered. The frizzes were already combed out damp. She parted off a strand of her brown hair, scrooched a little to look into the skimpy mirror and set the tongs just right, and began the meticulous winding of the strand upon the heated iron. So damp as it was, her hair would need a full minute perhaps for the curl to set. An idle minute, with nothing to do but hold the tongs steady and wait.

The footsteps were coming down the hall. Len turned her face toward the door, idly wondering whom it could be. The thin ingrain carpet could not deaden their sound, but the owner of the feet was doing his best to walk silently. From the sound, Len guessed that he was walking on his toes. And that was strange. Whoever had business down at that end of the hall certainly had no reason to come tiptoeing along in broad daylight. Len did not like the idea.

Her door was not locked. She never thought of locking a door except at night and in a strange place. She let the curl take its chance. She slipped the iron out of its hair cocoon and went over to stand by the door, making no sound whatever in her thin dress-shoes.

The man was coming slowly, apparently stopping at doors to listen. Len lifted her curling iron which was still pretty hot, and held it ready to poke into the fellow's face if he opened her door. She did not believe it was any range man. The town was full of strangers, and there had been a good deal of drinking and excitement over the betting.

Bing had said, when he brought up her suitcase, that the town was hog-wild over the races and the wrestling match. This might be one of the wild ones, she thought. And she told herself grimly that he would be wilder when she got through with him.

So far as she was concerned, it was a false alarm. At the door next her own the footsteps halted definitely. Len waited, expecting the other door to open, but instead she heard a faint tapping spaced in what apparently was some prearranged signal. Immediately a hinge creaked slightly.

"Oh, I thought you *nev*-er were coming!" breathed an agitated voice she had supposed was at that moment twittering inanities up in the grandstand. "I've simply died a thou-sand *deaths* waiting for you!"

Mysteries always exasperated Len Adams. Myrtle Forsyth certainly had left that room more than fifteen minutes before with her placid aunt, Mrs. Rogers. Len had heard her go down the hall, talking in her exclamatory fashion, and she had not heard her return; but naturally she had not listened. She had probably been at the window watching the street and taking due note of the fact that while the other boys mounted and rode away toward the stockyards, Bert Rogers' Flopper remained tied to the rail. Well, Myrtle was certainly up to one of her sly tricks. Len inclined her ear to the wall and listened frankly.

"I couldn't slip away before," whispered a man. (Len frowned and pressed her ear closer to the narrow crack at the edge of her ill-fitting door. Whispers are almost impossible to identify, as every one knows.) "I hired a fellow to take my stuff to the depot. Are you all set to go, sweetheart?"

Myrtle gave a suppressed giggle.

161

"I'm simply loaded *down* with clothes I was afraid to pack. I know I must look a perfect *fright* with two sets of underwear and goodness *knows* how many petticoats—you'll have to take me shopping the very first *thing*. I'm going to cost you an *awful* lot—"

"Say, what do I care? Stay with me and you can wear diamonds. I'll step out of this town with enough money—" Still that maddening whisper.

So Myrtle and the Native Son were planning to elope. Len lowered her cooling weapon and straightened with a scornful little smile. Miguel was such a nice boy, it seemed a shame he was really going to waste himself on a girl like Myrtle Forsyth. Myrt had dragged him into this sly business, Len was willing to bet anything. She half turned to resume her hair dressing when a sentence froze her to strained attention. With no compunction whatever, she glued her ear to the crack and heard every word that was spoken. It was easy enough. The Palace Hotel was a ramshackle frame building with thin board partitions, and in that empty upper floor the smallest sounds were audible.

The conference ended in a series of moist inarticulate sounds that brought a surge of crimson into Len's cheeks. She waited until the footsteps died away down the stairs, going as stealthily as they had come. She even heard the dining room door open and the tread of feet across the bare floor beneath her. He was going out the back way, and she needed no proof that he would presently appear innocently enough on the street in the vicinity of the blacksmith shop. Myrtle tiptoed from the next room, went from the lower hall into the hotel parlor, just as Len expected, and very soon was to be seen flitting across the street with her aunt, who no doubt had been asked to wait in the parlor for her. Mrs.

Rogers was a huge, inert woman who weighed at least two hundred pounds and never was known to exert herself more than was absolutely necessary. She could be entirely depended upon to seat herself in the largest patent rocker in the parlor and sway placidly back and forth until Myrtle came for her.

While her curling iron was heating again, Len discerned Myrtle's simple strategy. When the iron was hot she began to wind a strand of hair around the tongs and discovered that her hands were shaking. By the time she had blistered her forehead in two places she lost all interest in her hair. What difference did it make? She would keep her hat on anyway, until after the races, and she would have time to do her hair before supper.

Stabbing a long hatpin through her new white leghorn hat as she went, Len fled down the stairs, and without thinking of the unmaidenliness of it, pushed open the door to the barroom. An hour before she would not have dreamed of doing that, but neither would she have dreamed of laying aside her pride—some called it stubbornness—as she was doing now.

"Oh, Mr. Rogers," she called crisply, "may I speak to you a moment?"

To all appearances Bert Rogers was lounging against the bar, idly moving a mug of beer round and round in its own tracks while he talked with the bartender. In reality he was keeping an eye on the street as it was reflected in the bar mirror, and he was listening for a certain footstep on the stairs beyond the door. Yet he started with genuine astonishment when Len called him, and in a less vital matter Len would have snubbed him unmercifully for the blank amazement in his eyes as he hurried up to her.

"We've got to find the boys," she said in a fierce undertone, catching his arm and pulling him into the

163

empty dining room. "All of them—the Flying U outfit. Jump on your horse and beat it up there and round them all up, but for goodness' sake don't let on it's anything in particular. How can we manage it so I can talk to them without the whole town wondering what it's all about?"

"You want to do the talking yourself?" Bert's hand closed over her fingers on his arm.

"Oh, yes! I must, Bert. It—it's got to be handled with kid gloves—but it's got to be *handled*."

"I'll get the bunch together and bring them down for a drink, then. There's plenty of time before the real action starts; all those freak races don't amount to shucks. We'll ride down in a bunch, and you be walking along and meet us about halfway. Nobody'll be surprised if we stop and talk to you for a minute or two. How does that sound?"

"Fine, Bert. Beat it up there quick. I'll keep watch and start when I see you coming. Out there in the open—don't forget, will you?"

"Forget a thing you want?" Bert swept her into his arms. "Len girl—"

Two minutes were used; neither would have called them wasted. Then Bert was gone, and Len was left to straighten her hat and otherwise compose herself while she waited.

Evidently the Happy Family had scattered through the crowd, swarming beyond the stockyard wings. Len was growing very anxious, watching the few rods of trail up by the stockyard wings visible from the window where she stood. It seemed an hour before the well-known group of riders appeared, Bert Rogers in the lead.

Men headed toward cold beer on a warm day seldom took so leisurely a pace as these. They came on at a

164

walk. Len straightened her new hat again, patted the damp tresses of brown hair on her temples and hurried across the street, holding her flounced skirt daintily out of the dust.

Six mounted cowboys reining their restive horses to an uneasy stand before one slim girl so pretty as herself attracted more attention than Len had anticipated. Curious glances strayed that way and more than one straggler slowed his steps as he came near. Len had to make the meeting a brief one and she did. A charge of birdshot fired point-blank in their faces would scarcely have startled the Happy Family more than her first sentence.

"Nameless has sold you boys out," she announced without prelude. "He's going to throw the foot race. That Milk River bunch has promised him the purse and half their winnings to let Red Willis beat him, and they've paid him two hundred dollars to bind the bargain. For goodness' sake, keep your heads. If you jump him about it, he'll lie himself out, and so will they. You've got to figure out some way to prevent it, that's all.

"And another thing; Nameless and Myrt Forsyth are planning to take the five o'clock train for Helena and get married. Somebody ought to tell Miguel—only he'd try to kill Nameless and get himself in trouble. I was—" Len caught a warning signal in Bert Roger's eyes, looked the way his glance indicated, and saw two gangling youths stop to stare open-mouthed, waiting to drink in every word that was uttered. "I was just going to find the girls," she finished lightly, and caught her flounced skirt up at the side as was the fashion of that day. "Good luck—may the best man win!"

She was gone, and with a resentful glance at the two boys, the Happy Family rode on without a word.

165

HONESTY IS SLOW
TO SUSPECT

"Aw, that's just some josh of Len's," Happy Jack protested uneasily. "I betcha she made that up just to scare us fellers."

"She did not," Bert Rogers squelched him. "Wherever she got it, Len believes it, all right."

"I ain't a doubt in the world she fed that to us in good faith," Big Medicine conceded generously, "but it's a damn' lie. I don't care who told her. Nameless is as straight a boy as ever lived."

"I wonder," Chip reflected aloud, "if that happens to be Andy's idea of a joke. I haven't seen him or that Native Son for the last hour or so. Maybe he sprung that yarn on Len."

"Not with Mig around, he wouldn't. Not about that trip to Helena." Bert's tone was positive.

"No, but Andy's capable of saying anything. He and Len have been pretty friendly—"

"Say, lemme tell you fellows something. Len and I have made up. There's nothing between her and Andy, or anybody else. And I'll tell you another thing; she was all upset over this story, and wanted me to round you boys up right away, so she could tell you. She never mentioned Andy. Besides, she knows he's always playing tricks. She wouldn't fall for anything he could tell her."

They were by that time at the Elkhorn hitch rail, empty now of all tie ropes save those they were swiftly looping over the rail. Distant yells indicated the satisfactory completion of the first event before the grandstand, a potato race for boys under fifteen. The brass band from Havre struck up "El Capitan" march, drowning the scattered cheering.

"Well, let's go through the motions of a drink," Chip suggested. "We'll have to get back up there. Did she say who told her that yarn, Bert?"

"Not a word. She was going to, if them darned kids hadn't come along, trying to get an earful."

"I betcha that Milk River bunch is back of this," Happy Jack made another guess in the dark.

Big Medicine pounced upon it.

"By cripes, you can bank awn it, there's some dirty work back of that tale. They want us to pull down our money, or else force Larry off'n the track. Shore, that's what they're up to! They think we'll swaller all that, by cripes, and won't let 'im run. And throwin' that load about him takin' the five o'clock train with Myrt—why that there's just poppycock. He wrassles the Shelby Swede at seven. How's he goin' t' take the five o'clock train?" Big Medicine glared from one to the other as if they were somehow to blame for the accusation.

"You might ask him, Bud," Chip suggested.

"By cripes, I wouldn't insult the boy by even mentionin' sech a thing. Them skunks from the north is scared, that's all. Somebuddy's got wise to who our man is and they're tryin' to rib up trouble between us and him."

"Well, we'd shore be in the middle of a damn' bad fix if it was true, by golly." Slim had suddenly awakened to the portent of Len's story. "I got more up on that foot race than I c'n earn in a year, if I lose. Say, where's Nameless at? I'm goin' to ast him if it's so, by golly!"

"No, you ain't, by cripes!" On the very steps of the saloon, Big Medicine collared Slim and held him. "You ain't goin' to upset that there boy and create hard

167

feelin's right when he's got that race awn his mind. He's nervous as a thoroughbred hawse, by cripes. I seen him a few minutes ago, settin' up alone awn the fence, away back there by the north chute. I was goin' over to 'im but he flagged me back. He wants to be left alone, I tell yuh. He shore feels the responsibility—havin' all our money awn him. He—"

"Gee whiz, let's go and cheer 'im up, then!" cried Cal. "Leave 'im off there by himself like that—it ain't right."

"Come have a beer on me," said Chip, "and then we've got to get back up there. Bert, you see Len and find out where she heard that story."

"Trace it right back, and you'll find a Milk River man behind it," Big Medicine asserted loyally. "Nameless couldn't pull off a thing like that if he wanted to. He ain't been outa my sight all day."

Which only proves how honest a man may be and yet be far away from the truth.

They rode back to the field and found Andy, Miguel, Pink and Weary roosting in a row on top of the fence, enjoying themselves hugely with a buggy full of girls from the Marias country in the shade just below them. Just far enough apart from the group to give him an air of aloofness, Nameless was perched on a wide plank, watching all that went on. He waved a negligent acknowledgment of their hail, but his manner did not invite company, so they left him to himself. There was nothing wrong with Nameless; any one of them would have been willing to bet on his loyalty as they had on his speed.

Len Adams, too, was plainly visible but for the moment quite unattainable. Bert presently discovered her sitting near the top of the grandstand, with the Little Doctor on one side and Myrtle on the other, and all three were engaged in animated conversation. Rena sat just below Len, making a lively quartet.

Bert was some time in catching Len's glance, and when he had succeeded it did him no good. To his beckoning she merely shook her head and remained where she was, entrenched behind the crowd and seemingly engrossed with her companions.

"Take down your rope, why don't yuh?" bantered Cal, who was enjoying himself hugely at Bert's expense. "You oughta be able to cast your loop that far without snaggin' the wrong filly. Rope 'er and drag 'er down off'n her perch. You can bet your sweet life I would if it was me."

"I would for two cents," Bert retorted savagely. "She knows darn well I want to talk to her about something."

"Yeah, and so does the hull population of Montana," Cal chortled gleefully.

Whereupon Bert suddenly felt himself the unwitting clown of the whole show, and rode off red and furious, conscious of the hilarious laughter of the grandstand.

So the whispered revelation that had so disturbed Len fell upon practically barren ground instead of the fruitful soil she had intended and was taking for granted. From where she sat she could admire what seemed to her the consummate poise of the Happy Family. She never dreamed that their calm was the fatuous confidence of the ignorant victims of the plot against their peace and their pockets together, and she wholly misunderstood Bert's frantic efforts to call her to his side. She simply thought he was a young man delirious with love, and she was going to give him a piece of her mind for making her so conspicuous before everybody. Had she suspected the real urgency of the moment she would have trodden upon a multitude of toes to reach him.

169

So all her warning went for nothing, and events were left to move forward without let or hindrance, to the climax.

NO MORE DARK HORSES

FOR SOME REASON BEST KNOWN TO THE COMMITTEE, the horse races were held early in the afternoon. Probably the presence of so popular an athlete as Red Willis had a good deal to do with it, on the premise that star events should be saved for the last. The saddle-horse race put some extra money into the pockets of the Happy Family when Bert Rogers won with his horse Flopper, and every dollar was immediately wagered on Rufus Jones in the hundred-yard sprint against Red Willis and the Swede from Shelby. Len Adams would have been horrified to hear that, and to know that every bet the Happy Family offered was taken by some man from up Milk River way.

Big Medicine, looking more worried than his loud partisanship would seem to permit, at last rode over to where Nameless still perched in brooding solitude on the wide plank laid over the corner of a chute.

"C'mon, Rufus. Jar loose from them meditations and climb awn behind. I'll take yuh down to git your runnin' clothes awn. What's wrong with yuh t'day, anyhow? Sick?"

"I'm darned if I know, Bud." Nameless eased himself down to where he could slide a leg over the horse behind the cantle. "Ride around them crazy chumps, will you? I don't want to be held up for a lot of damned chin music."

"What's wrong?" Big Medicine repeated, reining

across the siding to ride down between the tracks out of the way of the crowd. "Ain't yuh well? You wanta buck up, boy. There ain't but a coupla more pony races, and then they'll just have to scrape and measure the track— and then, by cripes, we show Red Willis where to head in at! Lopin' Larry Jones, by cripes! You'll—"

"Oh, can that!"

Big Medicine twisted his big body in the saddle, but he could not see the face of Loping Larry Jones.

"Say, what's eatin' awn yuh, Rufus? Yuh don't mean t' tell me—"

"Bud, I'm all up in the air." Nameless seemed to let go all at once of his moody silence. "I'm so worried I'm fair sick at the stomach. I—"

"Say, if somebody has been runnin' off at the face about that damn' Milk River scheme to—"

"No, it's got nothing to do with Red's crowd at all. It don't concern nobody but me—and you fellows that have bet your good money I'll win that race. I've got to tell yuh, Bud—"

"Say, looky here, Nameless—"

"No, let me finish, can't you? I've got to say it. Ever since the band started to play and the crowd commenced to yell, I've had a queer feeling that I ain't any more Loping Larry Jones than you are."

"Hunh?" Big Medicine acted as if a bee had stung him. "*What's that?*"

"I've got a feeling I'm somebody else. Some darned amateur athlete that maybe took Loping Larry for his hero and tried to copy after him. I—well, I admit it sounds crazy, but that's the feeling I've got."

"That pitcher of Lopin' Larry was you," Big Medicine reminded him tersely, his mind working fast, though his words came with a gasp.

171

"It did look like me, a good deal," Nameless admitted, "but you want to remember that was all we had to go on. Just the resemblance. You all jumped to the conclusion it was me. Now—well, I just don't feel so sure. Still, I might be wrong. It's got my goat."

"That why you've been hangin' off by yourself and refused to talk to anybody?"

"That's it. I'm in a blue funk, if you know what that means. To think of all you boys have done for me, and the way you've backed me—why, if it should happen that I ain't Loping Larry but just some long-legged guy that looks like him—And if I ain't, we're done; that's all." His voice was heavy with despair. "It's going to take all the stuff Loping Larry's got to beat Red Willis. You know that yourself. I wish to God I *knew* what I could do. Why, I was so chesty, I wouldn't even let you watch me work out. I was so darn sure of myself—so sure I had my record all down in black and white—"

"What you need," said Big Medicine heavily, "is a shot of whisky. That'll take the kinks outa yore brain. Why—" he twisted again to make sure his words struck home "—Andy, he *knows* you're Lopin' Larry. He seen yuh run, and bet money agin yuh—and lost it, by cripes! Andy don't have to go by no pitcher in no paper. He *knows* yuh."

Behind his back Nameless was shaking his head with dismal uncertainty.

"If you've said once, I've heard you say a thousand times, that you wouldn't believe Andy Green under oath," he reminded Big Medicine. "I wouldn't go much on what he says."

Big Medicine only grunted in answer to that and reined his horse across to Rusty Brown's. They went in, and within five minutes they emerged, wiping their mouths on the backs of their hands.

"You trot over there and git ready, old-timer." Big Medicine's hand came down on the other's shoulder with a slap. "I'm right with yuh every step uh the way, don't you fergit that. I'm backin' Lopin' Larry, by cripes, and Lopin' Larry is shore goin' to bring home the bacon." He grinned his widest. "I'll wait right here for yuh," he added in a more casual tone. "Don't be long, Larry."

Fortified by further refreshment, they rode back along the railroad track the way they had come, but after that Big Medicine took care to ride where the enthusiasm was loudest. "Yuh see?" he bawled back triumphantly over his shoulder, as they loped past the grandstand to the clamor of at least five hundred pairs of clapping hands, "that there's for Lopin' Larry Jones. Even the women reckanize who yuh are, by cripes. I reckon them doubts of yourn are just about gone now, ain't they, Larry?"

"Just about," Nameless assured him, though his voice lacked conviction.

"Well, now, they better be, 'cause here comes yore turn right now. Here's the boys. Hang awn now, we ain't goin' to ride like we was goin' to no funeral."

He was right. The pace they took reminded nobody of a funeral as they dashed off, the Happy Family yelping at their heels. The Swede and his Shelby hackers had already arrived at the starting point, and across the scraped roadway a dozen Milk River boys convoyed Red Willis with whoops and jibes for the Flying U. Nameless slid to the ground and was immediately surrounded by his friends, each terribly anxious to give some priceless bit of advice which had just occurred to him.

Big Medicine waved them all back, leaned low over the neck of his horse and held Nameless with a steely clasp on his shoulder.

"Run like yuh always done awn that stretch uh trail over towards the Rogers place," he admonished. "They's a lot uh money awn you, boy."

"That's just what worries me, Bud." Nameless gazed up at him anxiously. "I told you boys not to take too big a chance on me."

"That's all right," Big Medicine grinned. "Don't yuh let that worry yuh for a minute. We ain't takin' no chance at all." He bent his bullet head closer. "We're backin' Lopin' Larry to *win*. Get that?"

Nameless drew back and gave him a quick, questioning look, glanced over toward the Milk River group and back again.

"I'll do my best," he said in a curious, half-defiant tone.

"Damn' right you will," said Big Medicine in a tone remarkably subdued for him.

"Come on, you loping lollypop," Red Willis suddenly yelled, hitching up his belt as he walked to the starting line. "Say, boys," he cried to the Milk River men, "that dark horse of the Flying U's looks more like a buckskin mule to me. Buckskin is that yaller shade, ain't it?"

A great laugh went up among Red's admirers.

"Nope," a Four-Eleven man caught up the jibe, "that dark horse over there is just nothin' but a wind-broken maverick the Flying U picked up on the range."

"Weanin' time comes early, up on Milk River," Pink made contemptuous retort in his clear treble. "Listen, and you can hear the calves bawlin' away down here."

"Yeah, there's going to be a heavy frost up that way," Andy predicted cheerfully. "Looks like a cold, hard winter up on Milk River."

At that moment the marshal of the day came jogging up on a white horse from the livery stable. Silence fell

174

abruptly, as if a door had slammed and shut out the tumult of the crowd. The Shelby Swede, a stocky, silent, young fellow with clipped blond hair, took the center of the track and dropped to one knee, still grinning at the caustic wit of the cowboys. Three feet away at his left crouched Loping Larry, slim, tense, poised for flight. And on the right the lean figure of Red Willis staring fixedly at the goal three hundred feet away.

Milk River men and the Happy Family alike edged off out of the way, holding their horses with tight rein, ready to follow, eyes glued to the runners. The marshal backed his white horse, waited until men's nerves were taut as fiddle-strings, raised his gun deliberately, aimed it at a small white cloud and fired the signal. As if released by some strong invisible spring at the sound, the three crouched figures shot forward and went streaking up the smoothed track toward the grandstand.

Fifty feet, a hundred feet—the Swede's shorter stride was dropping him inexorably behind. The race was between the other two and Red Willis was holding his own and a little better.

"Come on, Larry!" yelled the frantic Happy Family.

"Go it, Red! Beat that lopin' four-flusher!" roared the Milk River cowboys.

"Go on, Rufus! Fan it, Nameless!" A note of fear was creeping into the voices of the Happy Family. Gradually, almost imperceptibly at first, Loping Larry was dropping behind. Even the Swede was threatening to take second place.

Then suddenly Big Medicine, riding jealously close to the track, whipped out his six-shooter and fired. A spurt of dust flicked up three inches from Loping Larry's left heel. He lifted that heel in a tremendous forward leap.

175

"Run, you son-of-a-gun—*run!*" bellowed Big Medicine, planting another bit of lead where it would grow the most speed. "What'd I save yer life for? *Run!*" Another bullet lifted the heel it all but grazed. "Throw the race, would yuh? Sell us out, would yuh? *Run!*" Whenever he shouted "run," Big Medicine emphasized the word with a shot. "Steal Mig's girl, would yuh? *Run,* you son-of-a-gun! *Run!*"

Nameless did not exactly run, he flew. He leaped across the score line exactly six jumps ahead of Red Willis—one jump for every bullet from Big Medicine's gun—and he kept on going. By the time the Happy Family dodged hysterical humans and topped the brow of the little hill just beyond the stockyard wings, he had gone.

They galloped down the slope, looking for him, but he had disappeared utterly. They pulled up at Rusty's hitch rail, not because they meant to go in, but from force of habit. Not a soul was in sight. They could not even see the tracks of his spiked running shoes in the dust.

"Well," said Big Medicine, goggling this way and that, "he *run,* by cripes!"

"Mamma!" sighed Weary, "That boy's the lopin'est wolf that ever dodged a bullet."

"Yeah," grinned Andy Green, "the only reason that bird didn't take wing and fly, is because Big Medicine run outa lead."

"Well, by golly," Slim contributed ten minutes later, "about the only way to ketch 'im now is to round up a bunch uh them gopher-snarin' Blackfoot squaws and set 'em to watchin' them gopher holes this side the stockyards. They might be able to snare Nameless when he sticks his head out of a hole—I dunno."

176

"Aw, I betcha he'll dig a burrow clean over to the Missouri River," Happy Jack exaggerated Slim's wild theory. "He's liable to drownd if he pushes through below water line."

Len Adams, walking fast and forgetting all about her dainty flounced organdie, projected herself into the argument.

"If you're looking for any lost or strayed foot-racer," she said in her clear, vibrant voice, "you'll probably find him over to the depot, hiding amongst the freight till the train pulls in. I was up where I could watch him go. I had to laugh," she broke off to interpolate, bubbling with mirth. "I kept thinking about that hotel Chinaman when one of you boys scared his cat half to death. I know it isn't ladylike to say, but I kept thinking, 'Gee cly, watch 'im flew!'

"Anyway," she went on, when she could be heard above the cachinnations of the Happy Family, "Nameless certainly flew. He ducked around the fence and ran crouched down in all those weeds till he got to the track, and there he wriggled out of sight between two box cars. I didn't see any more of him. Myrtle was walking all over my feet, in a hurry to get down out of the grandstand, and she headed straight for the depot too. The rest," she added, with a pretty little gesture of finality, "if your heads are working, you can maybe guess for yourselves."

Big Medicine's face went blank and turned a pasty color, so that every pockmark showed with pitiless distinctness. He whirled upon the Native Son and transfixed him with his pale, froglike stare.

"Say, Mig, that damn' skunk is figurin' awn runnin' off with yore girl," he bellowed hoarsely. "Wasn't enough, by cripes, to fetch smallpox onto the ranch and

177

make all the trouble he could between us—wasn't enough to try an' sell us out to that damn' Milk River bunch—he's got t' play a lowdown trick like takin' a feller's girl and runnin' off wither.

"How about it, Mig? Just say the word, and by cripes, I'll go kill that dirty whelp m'self. If you want Myrtle, by cripes, you're goin' to have 'er, if I have to' drag 'er over here like I'd drag a yearlin' to the brandin' fire. I'll stand fer a lot, by cripes, but—"

"Let them go," said the Native Son, and laid a friendly, detaining hand on Big Medicine's arm. He could feel the muscles quiver with the intensity of Bud Welch's emotion. "Let him have her. It's all right with me, *amigo*."

"Shore yuh don't want 'er yoreself?" Big Medicine stared anxiously into his face. " 'Cause if yuh do—"

"Would you?"

For a long minute the two looked deep into each other's eyes. Their faces relaxed. When the gaze broke, eyes and lips were smiling in perfect understanding.

"No, by cripes. I'd call it a good riddance to both of 'em. They done nothin' but make trouble ever sence they set foot awn the ranch."

"You said it, *amigo*."

"Well," Pink snapped impatiently, as he swung to the saddle, "we got all the time in the world, of course—but I'm going to rake in my winnin's before that darn Milk River bunch gets outa town!"

"And when you've collected," Len called after them, "don't forget the goose that saved Rome!"

"Say, what kinda candy does that little goose like best?" Andy inquired over his shoulder, as he reached for the bridle reins.

"Never you mind what kinda candy," Bert Rogers

178

served masterful notice to them all. "I'll be buying the candy from now on."

With a clatter of hoofs and a flurry of lifting dust, the Happy Family rode blithely away up the slope. One exuberant young man looked back to wave his hand at the smiling girl who watched them go. And in the lead of the galloping cavalcade rode Big Medicine and the Native Son, their voices mingling in eager talk as though they had just met after a long separation.

We hope that you enjoyed reading this
Sagebrush Large Print Western.
If you would like to read more Sagebrush titles,
ask your librarian or contact the Publishers:

United States and Canada

Thomas T. Beeler, *Publisher*
Post Office Box 659
Hampton Falls, New Hampshire 03844-0659
(800) 818-7574

United Kingdom, Eire, and
the Republic of South Africa

Isis Publishing Ltd
7 Centremead
Osney Mead
Oxford OX2 0ES England
(01865) 250333

Australia and New Zealand

Bolinda Publishing Pty. Ltd.
17 Mohr Street
Tullamarine, 3043, Victoria, Australia
(016103) 9338 0666